PUMPKIN
SPIRITS

PUMPKIN SPIRITS

CANCEL

MARK MILBRATH

Nightforest Press

Copyright © 2016 Mark Milbrath

Published by Nightforest Press.
ISBN:9780997895476
ISBN: 0997895470

Editor: Summer Dawn Laurie

Cover Art © 2016 by Laura Diehl
www.LDiehl.com

TABLE OF CONTENTS

Prologue: The Seed Reader · vii

April's Storm · 1
The Ol' Crone and Her Gnomes · · · · · · · · · · · · · · · 11
Seeds, Needles, Bat, and Bones · · · · · · · · · · · · · · · 19
Ambrose and the Dead Pumpkin · · · · · · · · · · · · · 31
The Pipin' Mad Scarecrow · · · · · · · · · · · · · · · · · · · 41
The Serum · 51
The Clock-Fix Curse · 61
My Mom, the Undertaker · · · · · · · · · · · · · · · · · · · 73
The Nightmirror · 83
Maggie and Maglich · 97
The Creeper Train · 107

The Visitor· 119

Tricker? Or Treater? · 129

Epilogue · 139

About the Author · 141

PROLOGUE: THE SEED READER

I collect the stories of dead spirits. I listen to them here, in the Pumpkin Room. Welcome.

Every year on Halloween Night someone like you finds a way through the dark forest to my mansion. You hear the wind howling through the tree branches. You see the moon in the sky. It follows you. It watches you. Then, the bravest of you pass through the two stone pillars and walk along my lantern-lit path. You thump the iron ring against my heavy door.

You've been warned to stay away but you're too curious about me. You've heard that the dead tell me their darkest stories, usually of spooky things that happened when they were alive. And I preserve those stories. You've also heard that I travel the world in search of only the most ghoulish and sinister tales to further my collection.

My mansion is dark. I prefer it that way, but I give you a lantern. You follow me into the Pumpkin Room, my library, a carved-out orange orb. You gaze at the thousands of pumpkin seeds that adorn the walls like stars in the night sky. These seeds are my story collection. I am the Seed Reader.

Pick a story, I tell you. You shine the lantern about until you settle on one of the seeds. Once I retrieve the seed from the soft orange wall, it opens much the same way as a book. You sit in the center of the room in a chair made from dead fall leaves. Before I read the story, I ask that we make a pact: I agree to share a spooky story or two with you, while you agree that if I seek you out in this life or in the spirit world beyond, you'll share a spooky story with me.

Why, you ask? I remind you that I have devoted my entire life to collecting...*evil*...stories. *It is what the Seed Reader does.*

But what if nothing frightening ever happens to me? You wonder.

The candle burning inside of your lantern jumps, making eerie moving shadows along the walls.

It will when you least expect it. It has happened to everyone who has come here. No one has ever left the Pumpkin Room the same.

You sit quietly. Part of you wants to leave. You glance at the door.

Do we have a deal?

APRIL'S STORM

I promised an old and dear friend—let's call him Dustin—that I would keep this story to myself. But since he hasn't returned my phone calls and I no longer know his whereabouts, I don't think he can hold me to my promise. And truthfully, it is too interesting a tale to keep quiet any longer.

To begin, everyone has a 'schmirkle.' Some people hate the sound of fingernails on a chalk board. For others it is bees buzzing, spiders, fear of heights, or any number of things. My friend Dustin's schmirkle was Halloween.

Halloween reminded Dustin of the past, of being a kid sitting alone inside the living room looking out the window as all of the other kids were in costumes holding candy pails and trick-or-treating. Surely, he *should* have been out doing the same. But sadly, Dustin was an only child and his parents were usually too busy working or fighting and Dustin was often forgotten. His parents had never once taken him trick-or-treating. He had never experienced the joy of wearing a costume.

Let me also mention that Dustin grew up to be a bit of a celebrity. He was the man who delivered the weather on television at night. A necessary tidbit as we begin the story.

As mentioned, Halloween brought back painful memories for Dustin so once he had a house of his own and Halloween night came along, he didn't want to hear the doorbell ring and have to hand out candy to trick-or-treaters. So every year, he'd simply shut off all the lights and lock the doors. Then, he'd get in his car, grab a burger (*sans* mayonnaise) and fries from a drive-thru and head out into the mountains. Being in nature, alone with the sky, helped him forget these sad memories.

On this particular Halloween, Dustin's car rumbled and grumbled up the steep and narrow mountain road.

When rain began to fall, Dustin turned his headlights on. When the rain changed to snow, Dustin thought it would be wise to drive back to town—better safe than sorry. Dustin chuckled at the thought of the local weatherman getting stuck in a snowstorm. That would, no doubt, be bad for his reputation.

As he guided his car down the mountain, in the rear-view mirror came a sudden flash of red. What an odd color to see amid white snow and evergreens! Dustin instinctively slowed his car to a halt and craned his head around to look out the back window. What he saw... well, there was simply no explanation. He blinked and looked again. Sure enough, standing off to the side of the road was a small girl, maybe 10 years old, dressed in a long, red parka. Her stocking cap was covered in freshly fallen snow. And she just stood there, watching Dustin's car.

Dustin shifted the car into reverse and backed up until he was right beside her. Other than a little shivering, she stood still, just staring at him. Dustin got out of the car.

"Hey, uh, do you need help?"

"I'm cold," the girl said.

"I'm not surprised. What are you doing out here by yourself?" Dustin held out his cell phone. "Well, why don't you get in the car for a few minutes while we call your parents?"

The girl got in the car, still shivering, and Dustin cranked the heater dial on the dashboard. "What are you doing all alone out here in the middle of, well, a snowstorm?"

The girl pointed outside and said, "My bike is broken."

"Wait, you were *biking* in this?

"I just wanted to trick-or-treat. It was only raining when I left home but when the snow started falling on the road I skidded and fell."

"All right, well, use my phone and let your parents know you're okay. I'll go get your bike and give you a lift home," Dustin said before going back outside.

Behind a couple of pine trees, Dustin found the bike, or something that resembled a bike. The handlebars and frame were twisted into something that looked like a pretzel. One of the tires was flat and the other was under the snow a few feet away. Dustin popped the trunk and tossed the corpse of the bike inside.

"I'm afraid you're gonna need a new bike," Dustin said when he got into the car. "You must have been going pretty fast to have mangled..."

"You're Dustin, right? I recognize you from doing the weather on TV. I'd never get in a *total* stranger's car. My name is April."

"Well, nice to meet you, April. Yup, I'm weatherman Dustin. Look, the roads aren't going to get any better, and

I really need to get you home and then head for home my-self. What did your..."

April interrupted again. "They aren't home, as usual." She handed Dustin his phone back.

"Okay. Tell me where you live." Dustin shifted the car into gear.

"Please, please, please don't take me home. Nobody's there and it's...it's so lonely." April started to shiver and something told Dustin it wasn't just from the cold.

"April, I really don't have a choice. I must take you home. Where exactly are your parents?"

"Working or *out* somewhere. I promise they have no idea where I am and they don't care! Please don't make me go back there!" April started to cry.

Dustin rubbed his forehead and exhaled. His gas gauge read a little over a quarter of a tank. If he didn't take her home, he could be accused of kidnapping. The sun was set-ting quickly, plus the snow was falling harder, which meant the roads were becoming dangerous. He needed to head back toward home and soon.

"I'm sorry, April," Dustin said lifting his foot off the brake. He slowly drove down the mountain soon noticing lights and a few clusters of houses off to the right. In short order, he saw a road that curved in this direction.

"You must be this way, right, April?"

April nodded. Dustin felt a dull ache in his chest as she continued to softly weep.

Splatters of rain mixed with snow on Dustin's windshield.

"Why is it doing that? Raining and snowing together?" April asked.

Dustin loved to talk about the weather and was happy to answer her questions. When April asked how he was able to actually predict the weather, Dustin pulled a nickel out of his pocket and gave it to her.

"Heads for snow, tails for sun! It's that simple!" April burst out laughing and Dustin chuckled too. He liked her and felt an unexplainable connection to the girl.

"There is my house, on the corner," April said, suddenly pointing her finger to the right. Dustin's car skidded on the slush as he quickly braked. The tiny house didn't have any lights on inside. There was no garage and no cars were in the driveway. The house clearly was in need of a paintbrush and the grass hadn't been cut in a long time. A jagged crack lined the glass in the front window.

"Please don't leave me here," April again pleaded. Her voice cracked like the glass in the broken window. "Take me trick-or-treating, Dustin. Please, just a few houses and then I promise I will go home!"

Dustin shuddered. He had actually forgotten it was Halloween night. And you remember how he felt about *that*, don't you? But he also didn't feel right about sending her into that dark house alone. He wondered how severe the consequences would be for what he was about to do.

"I'm afraid you can't go trick-or-treating without a costume," Dustin said.

April's watery eyes widened and sparkled. She opened her long red parka to reveal a black dress, cape and tights. A pointed black hat was inside a coat pocket and a kid-sized broom sprouted from somewhere in her coat. An orange plastic bag from her pocket unfolded into a pumpkin candy pail.

No wonder she fell off her bike, Dustin thought to himself.

"I've always wanted to go, you know, trick-or-treating," April said putting the hat on and adjusting the broom.

"Wow, April," Dustin smiled. "You are full of surprises! Well done on the costume." He paused and let out a big sigh. "Okay, but seriously, just a few quick houses and then I need to get you home."

April playfully screamed and hugged Dustin. An instant later, she was out of the car and running up to a house. Dustin followed her as she went to each of the neighboring houses, shouting "trick-or-treat!" at every door.

April held Dustin's hand as they walked.

"I'm having so much fun!" April pulled Dustin up the walk to the next house. "Hold this for a sec." April put the candy bag into Dustin's hand. Then she rang the doorbell and hid behind him.

A woman answered the door and Dustin stood looking at her like a deer in headlights.

"Go on!" April nudged.

"Trick-or-treat?" Dustin whispered.

"Hmmm...you could have at least put on a costume, Weatherman. It would have been nice to have known in advance about the snow too." She dropped two candy bars in the bag and shut the door.

April laughed uncontrollably and then jumped about in fits of joy. Dustin tried not to smile but a grin broke through. He couldn't help it.

"April, I never really cared for Halloween but this is for sure a good Halloween memory," Dustin said as they slowly walked back to the car.

"And thanks to this nickel you gave me, I'll always be able to predict the weather!"

When they got back to April's house, Dustin was relieved to see a light on inside.

"Well, here you are. Look if you ever need anything you can..."

"Goodbye, Dustin," April said, scurrying through the falling snow to the front door. She didn't look back or even wave. Dustin wondered if he had upset her somehow.

Sadly, Dustin got in his car and put the key in the ignition. In a flash, he recalled that April had forgotten her bike in the trunk. He grabbed his coat and followed April's footprints in the snow up the walkway.

He knocked gently. Strangely, no one answered. He knocked harder. The door flung open until the security chain caught. There stood an older woman. Dustin could smell liquor on her breath.

"Hello ma'am…You must be April's mother. She ran off without her bike. I have it out in…"

"That some kinda sick joke, mister?" the woman slurred, eyebrows furrowing.

"Look, ma'am, I am really sorry. Perhaps I shouldn't have let her go trick-or-treating but when we got here there was no light on inside…"

"How dare you!" she snarled. "Comin' out here on the 'versary of my April's dyin'. You can visit her down at the end of the street if you'd like to pay respects. Do not EVER come here again!" The woman slammed the door. Through the closed door, Dustin heard the woman sobbing.

Dustin walked back to his car and opened the trunk. The bike had vanished. Confused, he checked his cell phone and saw that no outgoing calls had been made since the morning. He felt as if a bomb had exploded in his head. Instead of heading home, he drove in the direction the woman pointed. The road dead ended at a cemetery.

Grabbing a flashlight from the glove box, he walked amid the snow-covered gravestones. When he saw the pile of candy bars, suckers, and lollipops, his breath stopped. A shiny nickel sat atop the candy mound, which sat atop a grave. The headstone read: April Storm, beloved daughter: July 29, 1981 – October 31, 1991.

Dustin exhaled deeply. His eyes stung as he picked up the nickel and put it in his coat pocket. He would never part with it again.

THE OL' CRONE
AND HER GNOMES

I was given a story once about an unusual old woman. She lived at the end of a long and wooded street in a little orange house. Now, I say the word *unusual* to avoid using words like strange, or odd, as I have never met her personally, and don't want to seem judgmental. But, everyone thought it strange that she was so rarely seen, just once a week when she left her house to walk to the grocery store, which she did every Wednesday at precisely the same time.

She would push her very own grocery cart down the street. Inside the cart rode a single garden gnome painted with an orange hat and blue vest. She spoke to it as she pushed the cart. The cart clanked and rattled with so much noise that what she said to the gnome was a mystery. When she returned home from the store, she placed the gnome in her garden and then went inside the back door with her cart and groceries.

Her neighbors were a bit suspicious of her—maybe even frightened—as the old woman kept only to herself and seemed to like it that way. She didn't own a car or a telephone. She didn't even have a mailbox.

Ah, but what a garden she had! It covered the entire front yard and spread around the house to the back. It resembled a jungle. Plants were tall with long leaves; colorful flowers of many kinds bloomed everywhere. When autumn came, her pumpkins grew larger than any of the neighbors'. The lush greenery added to the mystery; she had never been seen weeding or trimming or fertilizing—or even picking a flower.

Now, there were two mischievous boys living in her neighborhood. Their names were Steven and Patrick and they were bullies of the worst kind. They'd been known to put sharp nails on their teachers' chairs and hurl water balloons at small children. For this quiet elderly woman, who clearly liked to be left alone, things were about to change. These devilish boys decided they simply didn't like her.

A few nights before Halloween, they dressed in all black and hid beneath the weeping willow tree across from the old woman's house. Their hope? Scare that "weirdo-woman" so badly that she'd have a heart attack, or at the very least move out of town.

Sticking to the shadows beyond the light of the lone street lamp, they snaked across the street and followed the narrow crooked walkway to the steps of her front door. The old woman's house was dark, less one small candle glowing behind a curtain. Steven went to the front door and Patrick went around to the back door. The moment he heard Patrick pounding on the back door, Steven thumped his fists hard on the front door. They each counted to 20, then sprinted back across the street to the willow tree.

When the old woman's front door flew open, the boys stifled their snickers. She shouted, "You can bang on my doors all you wish, but be warned: Stay out of my garden and keep away from my pumpkins!"

"We're not scared of you creepy ol' crone!" Steven shouted. The boys high-fived and scurried home.

The next afternoon, the bullies broke into a farmer's barn and stole enough corn to fill several pails with the hard kernels. Late that night, they snuck up the old woman's front steps. The candle again burned behind the curtains. Quietly, the boys set their heavy pails down and filled their hands with corn. On the count of three, they launched handful after handful at her windows. The kernels rat-tat-tatted against the glass. Perhaps the old woman thought she heard a freak hailstorm or even bullets from a machine gun.

With their pails empty, the bullies retreated across the street in fits of laughter.

"Dare ya to come out ol' crone!" Patrick shouted.

Like the night before, the old woman opened her front door. "You can bang on my doors and throw corn at my windows all you wish, but be warned: Stay out of my garden and keep away from my pumpkins!"

Patrick laughed so hard he nearly peed his pants while Steven fell to the ground wheezing delightfully.

The next day, the old woman left her house. But it was not grocery Wednesday and she was not pushing a cart. She did, however, have her garden gnome with her, carried tightly in both arms. One by one she went knocking on her neighbors' doors in the hopes one of them might be able to help her with the bullies. Not a single person came to the door. Suspicious and anxious, most simply hid behind window drapes and watched through a crack until she left. After all, what could that unusual lady who lived in the orange house (clutching that silly garden gnome) actually want?

Once everyone was asleep that night, the night before Halloween, Steven and Patrick waited under the willow. This time they had only one bucket and it was filled with water. Across the street, the candle flickered feverishly behind the curtain. Sneaking onto her porch, the boys hung the water pail from a hook that was probably intended for a bird feeder or plant. They tied the pail to the doorknob. When Steven knocked on her door, his voice was filled will suffering.

"Oh, please, help me! I have fallen and hurt myself! I need a bandage...and some water!" Steven said through a devilish grin.

When they heard footsteps coming to the door, the bullies jumped into the tall bushes at the front of the house to watch their prank unfold. The instant the old woman opened the door, the bucket tipped and drenched her with cold water. As the door opened all the way, the rope pulled the bucket off the hook so it landed painfully the top of her head. Staggering to her knees, water dripping from her face, the old woman looked out across the street to the willow.

"You can bang on my doors and throw your corn at my windows and dump water on me all you wish, but be warned: Stay out of my garden and keep away from my pumpkins!"

On Halloween morning the old woman once again went knocking on neighbors' doors, with her garden gnome of course. She continued all the way to the police station on the other side of town for help (they thought she was a bit loony) only to be told that she needed proper identification like a driver's license (which she didn't have of course) in order to get local police help. The town had officially rejected her.

When nighttime came and all the kids had returned home from trick-or-treating, Patrick and Steven again waited under the willow with a plan for an especially sinister act.

They once more crossed the shadowy street; the candle behind the curtains flickered violently back...and forth. Back...and forth. For their opening act, the boys went trouncing through her garden, tearing out colorful flowers by the roots while their boots destroyed majestic plants that had been growing for years.

Soon, it was time for the main event. Steven pointed toward the giant pumpkins and seconds later both bullies were on their knees, each wrapping their arms around a gourd. The moment the boys started to lift the pumpkins off the ground...

The candle behind the curtains suddenly went out and the garden fell into an eerie darkness. The hairs on their necks stood at attention and icy chills shot down their spines. Something was happening.

The boys' mischievous grins turned into mouths gaping open in terror. Their eyes bulged wide as they witnessed every pumpkin in the garden tilting in unison, their stems pointing in accusation directly at them. The boys' arms went slack, softly releasing the pumpkins back to the ground.

As the boys stood, something shifted. The pumpkins looked even bigger. So did the flowers. In fact, the entire garden seemed to be growing. Until they noticed their clothes hanging loose. In fact, it was Steven and Patrick who were shrinking! Fear -or something worse—had frozen them in place; unable to move, the bullies watched with wide, unblinking eyes as the jungle soon towered above them. Their limbs went rigid, mouths sealed shut, eyes blank stares of terror.

By late the next day, word had spread to everyone in town to be on the lookout for Steven and Patrick, as they had not returned home from trick-or-treating the night before.

But that wasn't all everyone was talking about. The next morning, all the town's Halloween jack-o'-lanterns and pumpkins were missing. Every single one was found on the property of the old woman who lived in the orange house at the end of the street—in the garden, on the walkway, even dangling from the tree branches. The ones with the biggest and brightest carved smiles were on the rooftop facing out to the street. One popular explanation was that the missing boys, known for being mischievous, must have played a prank on everyone. But where were they? How did they do it?

Weeks later, the boys were still missing. The old woman, meanwhile, had fallen back into her routine. Wednesdays were still Wednesdays and she still pushed her noisy grocery cart to the store at precisely the same time. Though there was one difference worth mentioning: she now had three garden gnomes riding inside the cart.

SEEDS, NEEDLES,
BAT, AND BONES

Tristine, Christine, and Nadine were bubbly happy girls and if you asked them about growing up in an orphanage, they'd show you huge smiles and tell you that it wasn't all bad. Sisters they were, each with long, straight blond hair. Their mother and father passed away in a car accident shortly after Nadine was born and they had been confined to this rundown orphanage since.

They were a package deal, so if you wanted one girl you had to adopt the other two. At the time of this story, Tristine was 12, Christine 9, and Nadine 7; old enough that there was little hope of ever leaving the orphanage. Who would want to adopt three not-so-young children?

But, I digress. Our story begins on Halloween Night, which was nothing to get overly excited about. Dressing up in costumes and trick-or-treating simply weren't part of this orphanage's activities. But a board game and laughter passed the time, until it got late and Mistress Matilda opened their bedroom door and gruffly insisted the three girls go to bed.

Two of the sisters did just that, but Christine was not tired. Instead she sat quietly, looking out the window, letting her mind wander a bit as she sometimes did at night. Three floors down, the streets were quiet; it was far past trick-or-treating time. Jack-o'-lanterns softly glowed on the porches and doorsteps of some of the houses.

Out of the dark, a long sedan pulled up and stopped in front of the orphanage. Christine watched as the passenger side window rolled down and a black cat jumped (or was it perhaps thrown?) out and onto the grass. The cat turned its head; its bright golden eyes peering *directly* up at her. The car sped away.

An animal lover, Christine didn't understand how someone could simply dump a cat. And this one had such pretty golden eyes—eyes that remained fixated on her. Christine shivered. Why was it watching her?

And what did it want? It *wanted* something. Maybe it was hungry? She simply wouldn't be able to sleep knowing there was an abandoned cat outside.

Meow...

At the sound, Christine decided to sneak out and do her best not to wake Matilda, who could be very cruel to anyone caught wandering *inside* the big house after hours. Nobody *ever* sneaked *outside* the house.

Tristine and Nadine were sound asleep and didn't hear their sister open or close the bedroom door. Two flights of wooded stairs were tricky to navigate in the dark but she'd walked them so many times she was able to avoid most of the creaks and groans, even in the absence of light. She carefully opened the heavy front door and made her way out onto the lawn.

The cat was still there, paws outstretched in the grass. It didn't look startled or surprised to see Christine walking toward it. *Meow.* Two golden eyes slowly blinked.

Christine tiptoed toward the cat, hoping not to scare it away. When she was close enough, she knelt and extended her hand. "Come here kitty cat. I won't hurt you. You need a warm blanket and some milk."

She was just about to touch the cat when it bounded away into the thicker grass behind the orphanage. Its golden eyes shone like little moon beams on the ground creating…a path.

Meow. It beckoned her.

Those eyes, Christine thought. *It wants something. But what?*

She followed the cat into the backyard, and when it skipped away toward the park, Christine continued to give chase, calling for it to stop. But every time she got close, the cat would scamper off.

Christine had never been this far from the orphanage on her own. Somewhere beyond the park was a swamp and she had heard Matilda say once that children who went there were never heard from again. But Christine was compelled to follow the cat. Just for a little bit longer. Certainly, she'd only be in the swamp for a second.

The grass turned to reeds almost as tall as she was and the ground became gooey, a cold milkshake of mud oozed through her toes. With each step forward, the ooze got thicker and her feet sank a bit deeper. She wondered if this is what quicksand felt like, just before it pulls you down into the abyss. Suddenly, she lost sight of the cat.

"Here kitty! Where are you? I'm gonna go back home if you don't come out now."

Christine coaxed her feet one more step forward, sinking nearly to her knees into the muck of the swamp. Now that she wasn't able to pull her legs free from the muddy goop, she began to panic.

At her scream, the cat's golden eyes suddenly re-appeared. And this time when it blinked, it began to... change. The cat's eyes grew to the size of golf balls. Its body elongated and stretched upward, quickly becoming as tall as the long swamp reeds. Its black fur morphed into clothing—a black dress, a hooded cape. And what were once two soft kitten ears became a tall, pointed hat.

Stuck in the muddy ooze, Christine could only watch as the innocent looking cat she had followed changed into a tall, yet frail, old woman with a sagging face. Her golden eyes emanated evil as her lips naturally formed a foul scowl that stretched almost ear to ear. Behind her, a broomstick was slumped against a large black cauldron.

"How marvelous of you to visit me! We witches just love swamps you know, as there are so many goodies for spells and potions here. How do you like it so far?" The witch laughed in an awful gluttonous cackle.

Christine had managed to free one of her legs and was trying to maneuver the other so she could run when the witch shouted: *"RUMBA TUMBA!"*

Instantly Christine's legs froze in place. The lower half of her body no longer had any feeling. A spell!

"Going somewhere, Girly? Not yet I hope. Our fun is only beginning!" The witch cackled, a laugh so shrill it stung Christine's ears. Terrified and trembling, she pleaded to the witch. "Please, just let me go back to the orphanage."

"Not so soon, for I have brought you here to do something for me. And your life very much depends on it."

Christine reached her hands down into the muck thinking she might be able to free one of her legs from the spell.

"That won't work, my dear. Try anything else and I'll turn your arms into snakes!"

Christine lowered her head. She quietly sobbed.

"No need to cry yet, Girly. I'm on your side. Look up at the moon. See it in the sky? Well, I need you to bring me some things I require for a potion. And they must be in my cauldron before the moon sets. If you should fail me, you *and* your two sisters…will go *poof.*"

The witch pointed a bony finger at some reeds. "*RUMBA TUMBA!*" They exploded into tiny clouds of smoke. The witch shrieked with glee.

"Follow my exact words. I require seeds, needles, a bat, and bones. THAT is what I need." The witch closed her eyes and held her hands open to the sky. There was a distant rumble of thunder and the ground gently shook.

"You don't need me for any of those things," Christine pleaded. "You have magic and can…"

"I need someone with a pure and innocent soul to bring them to me. That is part of the potion. *My* soul is already filled with sin."

The witch focused her glowing eyes on Christine again. "So, bring me three pumpkin seeds from jack-o'-lanterns burning on this All Hallows Eve. I also require six very sharp needles and one bat." The witch flapped her arms up and down, black sleeves billowing out like wings.

"Oh, and I need a few bones, preferably from something dead."

The witch paused then winked.

"RUMBA TUMBA!" The paralysis in Christine's legs vanished. "Go now. Return to me with the ingredients before moonset."

Christine was relieved to be set free but terrified of her orders. Through tears, she whimpered, "I can't possibly..."

"GO NOW!!" the witch shrieked back.

Christine turned and ran from the swamp and the witch. Her heart hammered in her chest. All the way back to the orphanage she thought of the witch's threat. Oh her poor sisters...they would turn into smoke too. And it was all her fault! She should never have followed that cat.

Christine decided to wake her sisters right away and ask for their help. Would they even believe her? Back at the orphanage, she tried the front door, but it was locked.

The back door as well. She was stuck in the cold, the only light coming from a few jack-o'-lanterns glowing across the street. Christine remembered the seeds the witch wanted.

She quickly ran from house to house, searching the carved pumpkins. A cold sweat broke on her brow. There was only one house left to search in the neighborhood. The final house had three jack-o'-lanterns. She nervously, but carefully, reached inside each. The first two gourds were cleaned out. The third, however...score!

Three seeds in hand, she turned toward the orphanage when the headlights of an oncoming car flickered. The car slowed as it got closer. Christine crawled beneath a large pine tree to hide. If the driver saw her, he might call the police and she still had three more ingredients to find. Finally, the car drove on. She needed to get back into the orphanage to her sisters. But how? The front door was locked.

Dashing across the street, Christine remembered the cellar door near the garden. Using both hands, she pulled as hard as she could on the cold metal handle in the ground. The door groaned open to reveal a ladder. Christine climbed down into the dark. The cobwebs were so thick she felt like she was walking through a jungle of hair. *Eew!*

Feeling along the wall, she found another ladder and up she climbed. *There must be a door here...*

Flopping open a square door at the top of the ladder, she stepped into a dark, stale smelling room with small windows on the far wall. Slowly, her eyes adjusted and she picked out the green orphanage van and the crates holding their equipment for summer recreation day. The good news was that the door connecting the orphanage kitchen was unlocked.

I need to wake my sisters NOW...

Christine tiptoed quiet as a mouse, back up the creaky stairs. She felt along the hall wall for the doorknob and went inside to wake her sisters.

She told them every detail about the cat, the swamp, the witch, and the potion, and that the three of them might be "POOFED" into clouds of smoke in the next couple hours when the moon sets. Outside their bedroom, footsteps approached the door. The girls ducked under their covers, quiet as the dead.

When Matilda's footsteps finally shuffled away from the door, Christine whispered, "Tristine, what should we do?"

Tristine lit a small candle. "Well, we have the seeds and there should be needles in one of the bathroom closets up here. But a bat? And *bones*? Gosh, there just isn't enough time!"

Realization was setting in and the tears came. "Poor kitty cat," Nadine's voice choked. She picked a hair brush from her bedside table to comb through some of Christine's muddy hair.

"Gosh, Christine! You're filthy," Tristine noticed. "You're getting dirt and pine needles everywhere. Did you climb a tree?"

Christine looked at the mess on the floor. She reached out for a handful of the pine needles.

Needles...

Christine's looked at her big sister with eyes a-gleam. "You don't suppose that these needles would work, do you? I mean, they are just that: needles!"

Tristine shrugged. "Hmmm. I suppose. But we still need a bat."

"And a place to dig up some bones," added Nadine.

"Maybe we don't have to," Tristine stood up and put her hand over her mouth. "What if we roll them?"

"Roll them?" the other two asked simultaneously.

Tristine started rummaging through the closet. She pulled out a board game. "Dice! Sometimes people call them bones."

Christine's eyebrows lifted. "That's great! All the witch said I needed were seeds, needles, a bat, and bones. Then she got all weird and stared up at the sky. I have a little time still to find a bat and then maybe get back to the witch before moonset."

"You're not going alone," Tristine said, putting on some sneakers.

Nadine jumped to her feet. "The garage!" She said, well above the level of a whisper. "There's a bat in the garage."

Christine nodded and grabbed a flashlight from the dresser, and led her sisters, quietly and quickly, down the staircase, through the kitchen, and into the garage. She sifted through one of the crates and sure enough found a baseball bat. She handed it to Nadine.

"You've done it, Nadine. Now we have all the ingredients. Let's go!"

The night air was crisp and the moon was close to the horizon. Running through the long grasses behind the orphanage and then into the park, the girls made their way carefully into the swamp.

A frightful voice startled the sisters. "A bit too scary to come back by yourself, eh? Hello, Girlies! Did you bring my potion ingredients or are you ready to go bye-bye?"

"We have the seeds, needles, bat, and bones," Christine said.

"Wonderful, start with the seeds. Drop them in the cauldron!"

When Christine did so, the water in the cauldron began to bubble and gurgle.

"Perfect!" the witch said. "Good Girly! Now the sharp needles..."

Christine put the pine needles into the cauldron; large bubbles rose from the cauldron and into the air, gently popping.

"Now, the bat. Quickly, the moon is setting!"

Nadine produced the baseball bat from behind her back and dropped it into the cauldron.

The water from inside the cauldron started to bubble over, foamy white suds running down the sides and into the swamp.

"No! Not *that kind* of bat! You tricked me!"

Tristine quickly tossed the dice in the cauldron. Bubbly water exploded over the rim of the cauldron, splashing everywhere.

"Noooooooooooo! Those aren't real bones!" the witch howled. "Ruined! You ruined the potion." She began to choke, her words just a gurgle. A look of both fear and surprise came over the witch as she leaned over and began to shrink right before the girls' eyes. Her back hunched and her arms stretched to the ground and she quickly returned to her form as the cat with golden eyes. The cat hissed at the girls and scampered away.

"*Rumba Tumba,*" Christine whispered.

AMBROSE AND THE DEAD PUMPKIN

I am reluctant to share this story with you. It is disturbing, given to me by a boy who believed himself to be perfectly normal. (On a side note, it seems the people I've met who think themselves normal are usually those with too many loose screws to count). The one thing I will say about this poor child is that his genetics may have contributed to his woes. In any case, here is his story in his own words.

I was only 11 when *it* happened. *'It'* being the night that changed my life forever. Maybe I deserved it? Maybe I fell victim? I can't decide. And it doesn't matter now. Here's how I remember it.

My name is, well, *was* Ambrose Critcher and I was a totally normal kid. *Mostly* normal anyway. The biggest difference between normal and me is that I liked to break things. Ruin things. Destroy stuff. Especially the toys my parents bought for me. Even the electric train they got me for my birthday. Mom once described me as King Midas, except that everything I touched turned to junk instead of gold.

In my defense, I don't think my love of all things broken was totally my fault. I am pretty sure it was a family thing. Mom would sometimes break a plate or a cup on the kitchen counter for no apparent reason, and I'd sometimes spot Dad pounding old furniture or appliances in the garage with his sledgehammer. We were always out buying new things to replace our broken stuff.

Speaking of Dad, he was the one person I really wanted to be like when I grew up. Which is normal, right? He was really great at sports and got all As and Bs on his report cards. After school, he joined the Navy, stationed on a ship far away on the other side of the world. Eventually, he started his own business. And I'm pretty sure he had lots of dates in his glory days. Sometimes, my pop would talk about a girl from high school or something and Mom would get all upset. This usually happened at the dinner table, which was about the only time we were all together.

One late October evening at that very dinner table, after Dad had his standard ration of beer, he revealed something about his past that both Mom and I found astonishing. Staggering. He boasted that when he was my age—together with one of his friends—he roamed the town and smashed 99 jack-o'-lanterns during a Halloween season. Mom gave him a disapproving look. The same look she gave when he talked about pretty girls. Then she muttered something about a dead pumpkin and what probably happened to his pumpkin-smashing friend. Dad burped and said something about not believing in ghost stories.

I couldn't really hear them over my coughing as I had choked on my mashed potatoes. I couldn't believe the coincidence! The last several nights I had been sneaking out of my room and wandering the neighborhood doing exactly that: smashing jack-o'-lanterns. And just like my pop all those years ago, I was keeping count. Thus far, I had pulped 77 and October still had a couple more days to go.

Maybe you think I'm pretty low-life. I don't blame you. I said I liked to break things, but the first time I splatted a nicely carved jack-o'-lantern on the sidewalk, I was instantly addicted. To hear it "thunk" on the ground and see its insides scatter. Ruined. Smashed. Better than that train set.

I thought about what a thrill it would be to someday sit at that very dinner table, and, when Mom stepped out of the room, whisper to Dad that I had bested his old record of 99. That I had pulped 100! And I did it alone, without the help of a friend!

So, the night before Halloween, once my parents went to bed, I put on my coat and crept out my bedroom window. I remember it was unusually cold and windy. It was especially dark with no in the sky and I had a really long way to walk. See, I had already made pie filling of all the jack-o'-lanterns at nearby homes. I was glad when I finally spotted a few orange smiling faces glowing on the front steps of a house. One by one, I hurled them to the sidewalk. My insides tingled with each thump, squish, and splat. That brought me to 90. Ten more to go.

Within two hours, I was up to 97. My whole body tingled and buzzed. Three more to reach my goal. Staying in the shadows and using the trees for occasional cover, I searched. And searched. It was nearly midnight, but I wasn't going home until I splatted three more...

Eventually I spotted one, resting on the steps of a dark house. More like a shack. The lawn was unkempt with overgrown bushes and the roof was hanging over the front porch. The wind suddenly picked up and the trees began to sway in front of the house. I was a little creeped out. If it weren't for the jack-o'-lantern, I wouldn't have been able to see. Its candlelight made eerie shadows on the narrow walkway.

And you know that feeling you get when someone is staring at you? Well, I had *that* feeling. Big time. So, I kept myself alert and quiet.

By the looks of it, I'd be doing this jack-o'-lantern a favor by putting it out of its misery. Its skin wasn't pumpkin orange but more of a charred gray, with gross orange and green blotches. Sickly. Nasty. Ugly mold was caked around the stem. Lots of tiny cracks branched out from its triangle eyes and frowning mouth. I thought it looked like a zombie head. Evil. And it smelled stale and old, rancid, like it had been sitting on these very steps for hundreds of years.

With a deep breath, I reached out to pick it up...

Don't do it, Ambrossssssssssse.

The voice sounded like the hiss of a snake. I pulled my hands back and turned around. Where did the voice come from? My pulse raced.

Ambrosssssssssssse, pleasssssssse don't ssssspike me on the ground. I can help you.

The hissing, the voice, seemed to be coming from the moldy pumpkin on the steps. This had to be a trick. I took a deep breath and bent down to look inside the gourd. I thought I'd see some sort of speaker. Nope. Just a candle. It was bright too. Hurt my eyes to look right into it.

Ambrossssssssse, I know where you can find fresh jack-o'- lanternsssss.

This time, I actually saw the mouth move when it spoke. One of the droopy squinting triangle eyes jittered too. Then…it giggled. A gross, guttural, gurgly, goopy sound.

Heh Heh.

It started talking again and I really freaked out. This zombie-head jack-o'-lantern *knew* stuff about me. It *knew* that I'd been out pulping jack-o'-lanterns. It *knew* I'd reached 97 already. It *knew* Dad and his buddy had smashed 99 many years ago. AND it *knew* I wasn't planning on stopping until I had broken Dad's record.

Ambrossssssssse, I know you only need to smash a few more. Allow me to not be one of them and I'll help you.

I couldn't believe I was about to talk back to it. "I'll spare your life then." I thought the words I picked made me sound powerful even if they were lies. For, I fully planned on smashing it to bits and bits once I reached 100.

But first I had to pick it up. I held my arms outstretched as far away from me as I could. I was repulsed by it. I think *it* liked that.

Follow thisssss ssssssstreet.

I followed its directions and soon we were on the outskirts of town.

Clossssse now, Ambrossssssse. Acrossss the park.

There were homes on the other side of the park so this was a logical shortcut. The pumpkin was getting really heavy, and I could smell it rotting in my hands.

Heh Heh

That laugh was the last straw. We were smack-dab in the middle of the park but I didn't want to be carrying this rotten, reeking gourd anymore. "I'm gonna leave you right here and there'd better be jack-o'-lanterns at those houses or else I'll be back to make you a statistic." After I set it on the ground, I gave it a little "love-tap" with my foot. "Next time, it won't be so gentle," I said as I turned from it.

Heh Heh

Next thing I knew, I was flat on the cold, hard ground, my face now level with this jack-o'-lantern. Our eyes met and for the first time I got really scared. Something about the way it looked at me. A drop of ooze ran from the corner of its frown and its eyes were glowing...red.

I needed to get as far away as possible from the zombie-head and fast. But something was holding me down. My feet were caught. I tried to flop over and kick but something that felt like a belt was wrapping itself around my waist.

That's when I screamed. Uncontrollably. I tried to crawl away but something—ropes? snakes?—tangled around my legs and then my neck. I started to choke. Reaching up, I realized those somethings were vines: pumpkin vines!

This was no park. This was an empty pumpkin patch. The evil jack-o had lied to me. Deceived *me*. It brought me here on purpose. For fun or maybe for some kind of revenge. I didn't know. Was this the Dead Pumpkin thing Mom mentioned at dinner the other night? I twisted and turned and tried to jerk my body free but the vines held me fast. There was no escape.

All I could do was plead with the Dead Pumpkin. It was glowing brighter than before. So bright that it stung my eyes. I wanted to look away but I was fixated. Its mouth started to grow. And grow. There was a belching sound and orange slime spewed onto the ground. Pumpkin seeds shot like bullets toward my face. It was throwing up. This was easily The. Most. Disgusting. Thing. I had ever seen.

I watched the vomit spread out on the ground and begin to pool by my feet. The pool began to bubble until it exploded upward like a geyser. Pumpkin slime rained down until I couldn't see. It clogged my nostrils so I opened my mouth wide to breathe. Quickly, my mouth filled with goo. I was spitting. Gasping. Choking...

When I woke up, I was back at home! It was nighttime, and I was outside on the porch. But something was not right. The house had fallen into complete ruin: the porch had partially caved in, the windows were broken, and our garden was overgrown with weeds. There was litter everywhere. Where were my parents? How much time had passed?

It was when I tried to stand that I realized that Ambrose Critcher, the boy, was gone. I didn't have legs or arms. I just felt like a blob. Since I couldn't seem to move, I scanned the area for anything reflective.

A jagged piece of broken glass to my right. Looking deeply, I saw myself. I was...oh God. I had become the ugly, festering, moldy thing I had picked up that night before Halloween. I had become *the* Dead Pumpkin.

A girl and a boy were creeping up the sidewalk toward me. The girl had a sinister look on her face. The boy carried a hockey stick dripping with pumpkin guts. Instinctively, I knew what they had come for. And I was ready. As she reached down to pick me up...

Heh Heh...

THE PIPIN' MAD SCARECROW

When the woman introduced herself to me in an overseas airport lounge, I didn't recognize her at first. We hadn't seen each other in 10 years. Her husband had been one of my very best friends. When I lived closer, we spent a great deal of time together. But that was long, long ago.

She told me they had moved out of the city and gotten themselves a little farm way out in the country. She talked on and on about life on the farm—the roosters in the morning, the fresh air, the bonfires, the serenity of having no neighbors for miles. She probably would have kept talking of the farm had I not interrupted to ask how her two young daughters were doing.

She sighed, suddenly serious, and looked down at the floor, folding her hands to rest them on the small table. I was concerned. Something had happened to her little girls, something that was still unresolved. I couldn't imagine as to what it might be. Then she told me the disturbing story.

On weekends, Kaitlyn and Meagan just loved playing softball together outside. Meagan was nine years old and younger than her sister by two years. She couldn't throw the heavy ball very well, but she could sure swing a bat! One day I heard a loud crack and looked out the window to see a ball soaring over Kaitlyn's head, clearing the wood fence and sailing straight into the cornfield. With a THUD, the ball smacked the scarecrow square in its couch pillow face. Meagan was triumphant. It was the fifth time she had hit the scarecrow this fall. She'd remind her older sister of this feat whenever Kaitlyn teased her about not being skilled in the throwing department. Even the scarecrow seemed to celebrate, lurching gleefully back and forth on its pole; its left eye, a black button, no longer affixed to its face.

The girls ran to the cornfield to get the ball, but were having a hard time finding it. The corn was tall but the scarecrow was even taller; its shadow from the late afternoon sun darkened the ground. Meagan later told me she had the strange sensation the scarecrow was watching them.

I remember there was a sudden and strong gust of wind, and I heard Kaitlyn cry out. I knew that cry. She was hurt!

As I rushed up, Kaitlyn showed me the big, red scratch on her forearm. "The wind blew the scarecrow into me. The hay sticking out of its shirt is really sharp!"

The air had stilled, but the scarecrow continued to gently rock back and forth. Its mouth, a string of red yarn grinned mischievously. Hay jutted out from its torn overalls and faded blazer coat. An old gray tobacco pipe dangled from the side of its mouth, a hole poked in the stained couch pillow. Strange that it hadn't been knocked free even after the smack from the softball and that blast of wind.

Calling the ball lost, the girls decided to fetch another from the barn. So back over the fence we went, and right there, lying out in the open grass was the missing ball.

"How the heck did our ball get back out here?" Kaitlyn wondered aloud.

"Maybe the wind blew it back out?" Meagan said cautiously, reaching out to pick up the ball. Then she screamed and dropped it like a hot frying pan. The cover had been torn open and stuck to the innards was a button: the scarecrow's missing eye.

We all looked back out over the fence, up at the scarecrow gently swaying back and forth, its other button eye looking harmlessly nowhere. I decided it was time for dinner.

Over tater-tot casserole the girls told their father about the afternoon's adventure. He told them a story of his own about that very scarecrow.

"When we first moved here, I was out by the road and a garbage truck sped by. A pipe flew out the back and landed right at my feet. It was like the pipe knew it was going to a landfill and decided to escape. So, I put that very pipe in the scarecrow's mouth and crows haven't bothered our fields since."

The next day, while the girls were waiting by the highway for the school bus, I watched as Meagan nudged Kaitlyn and looked nervously back at the scarecrow in the cornfield.

When I tucked the girls in bed that night, Meagan pointed out the window and asked, "Is it just me, or is the scarecrow looking right at us?"

Kaitlyn studied it. "You're such a scardey cat! It isn't looking at us."

"I think it is," Meagan said. To settle them down, I said, "It's just a scarecrow, girls, something your dad put together from scraps and trash. Now, sweet dreams and nighty night."

The next afternoon, I was making a snack for when the girls got home from school. When I heard them calling for me, I rushed outside. They were clutching each other and pointing at the scarecrow. It was clearly in a different place in the cornfield than it had been yesterday, now closer to the house. I reminded the girls that their dad moved the scarecrow once in a while to fool the crows. What I didn't tell them was that he had been off the farm doing errands all day and I had no idea when he could have made the move. In any case, it satisfied their curiosity until lights out.

I had only just shut off my bedside lamp when I heard them calling.

"What's wrong?" I asked running into their room.

"We hear something tapping on the window glass," Kaitlyn whispered.

"It must be the scarecrow!" Meagan whimpered.

"Oh girls," I said. "It can't be. We're way up here on the second floor. Can scarecrows climb ladders?" I teased.

I sensed that words hadn't provided any relief. So, I drew the curtain aside and had quite a surprise. It turned out that the girls really did hear something tapping on the window glass.

"Shoo crow!" I said, scaring a big black bird off the window sill. "OK, nothing more to worry about." I snuggled with Meagan. Her heart was fluttering.

Finally Meagan drifted off but Kaitlyn was still moving around on the top bunk. I pleaded with her to go to sleep.

That was when a strange but familiar fragrance wafted in. I thought it smelled like burning cherries. It reminded me of my grandfather. It was the same smell as his pipe tobacco.

I must have nodded off since the next thing I remember is Kaitlyn whispering something about smoke outside, then yelling. "Mom, it's the scarecrow! Look out the window!"

Of course I insisted there was no silly scarecrow outside. To prove my point, I went to the window and saw exactly that: nothing. Just the dark farm as it always was at this hour. Still, I had no explanation for that smell of burning cherries.

"I know you are both frightened of something, but it's just in your heads. So I am going to sit right here at the window to keep you safe," I told them. I must have hummed a lullaby 50 times until finally they were asleep.

The next day passed uneventfully. But very early the following morning I woke to both girls' beds empty. Frantic, I looked everywhere in the house. I was about to call the sheriff when their father found them curled up together in the barn. Once I got them safe and calmed down, I demanded a full explanation.

"After we got in bed we heard more tapping on the window," Kaitlyn began.

"But we didn't want to wake you up again," interrupted Meagan.

"So," Kaitlyn continued, I went to open the curtain and saw another crow fly away. But what was really strange was the light on in the barn. We knew you and Dad had closed things up hours before."

"I thought it must be the scarecrow," offered Meagan.

"And I decided it was up to us to find out," said Kaitlyn. "We got out of bed, bundled up, and managed to pull open the heavy barn door. The barn was empty with just the flickering light bulb. It was pretty spooky but Dad must have forgotten to turn it off."

"Or maybe whatever turned the light *on* was there hiding in a dark corner," Meagan whispered.

"Then the barn door slammed shut behind us," Kaitlyn continued. "So we spun around and there was the scarecrow! He had our softball bat slung over his shoulder. He was grinning and his pipe was glowing red hot and smoke blew everywhere. It smelled like cherries."

Kaitlyn was shaking recounting what happened. I put my arm around her.

"We were frozen stiff as he pulled out a softball from his pocket and tossed it into the air. Then he swung the bat and...CRACK!" Kaitlyn said.

"I saw the ball coming, and I fell to the ground. It just missed my face!" said Meagan. "But he pulled another ball out of his pocket, and he hit Kaitlyn on her leg."

"I fell to the ground, it hurt so bad!" Kaitlyn said.

"The scarecrow hissed and then he tried to hit me again with another ball," Meagan said. "I felt it whoosh by my ear and it smacked the barn wall behind me."

I listened in disbelief. But they couldn't be making this up. The details were so unrehearsed.

Kaitlyn continued. "So, the scarecrow looked at me there on the ground and faster than the wind he was standing over me. My leg was hurting and I didn't think I could stand. He raised the bat high above his head. I thought I was going to die."

Meagan whined, "So, I found one of the balls and threw it as hard as I could. I hit him in the stomach but it didn't seem to hurt him."

"But it stopped him from clubbing me." Kaitlyn started to cry.

Meagan continued the story. "He wagged his finger at me back and forth in a scolding way. Then he pointed the bat at me...like I was next."

"Oh, sweetheart," I held both of my girls tight.

"Then the scarecrow got ready to smash me with the bat again. I covered my face with my hands. I screamed…I waited…but I didn't feel it. I heard a *hissssssssssssssss* sound that reminded me of that sound a rattlesnake makes," Kaitlyn said through tears.

Then Meagan continued, "I was so scared for Kaitlyn, so I grabbed the other ball he'd thrown at me and threw it even harder this time. I hit him! Well, I hit his pipe."

"It was her best throw ever," Kaitlyn smiled at her little sister. "She knocked that pipe right out of his mouth. And then the strangest thing…the scarecrow just fell in a heap on the ground next to me. It wasn't moving."

"Oh thank goodness," I said.

"But that's when we heard the flapping," Meagan said.

"The what?" I asked.

"I thought it was the scarecrow, maybe it had…come back to life or something." Kaitlyn said.

"But it wasn't the scarecrow," Meagan interjected. "It was…a bird! That crow! It swooped down and picked up the pipe on the ground and dropped it right on the scarecrow's stuffing."

"By the time Meagan had helped me stand up, the scarecrow had caught fire."

"There's a fire in the barn?" I interrupted.

"No, no. He burned really fast and we made sure to stomp out any embers. There was nothing but ashes left," Kaitlyn assured me. "It was so late and we were so tired."

And that's where their dad found them the next morning. I watched from the kitchen as the three of them walked out of the barn. I was so relieved that they were all right. After they told me everything, they took baths and then an afternoon nap. When I heard them both screaming, I ran upstairs to find both girls staring out the window.

Out in the field, their dad had built a new scarecrow. This one had a pillowcase face of pink and blue flowers and wore an old sun hat of mine and ripped jeans from Goodwill. I thought she looked rather sweet. Though, something did seem a bit odd.

"Mom, where did Dad get that pipe?"

THE SERUM

There are those who walk among us who aren't who—or what—they appear to be. After hearing this story, you will understand what I mean. And you may want to keep your eyes peeled from now on.

Now, unlike any of the other stories in this collection, I don't precisely know how this one ends! You see, years ago, someone brought me the 18-ounce plastic bottle of Pepsi you're about to hear about. Inside the bottle was not soda, or "pop" depending on where you live, but several pages of notes written by a boy who was in quite a bad predicament. I've pieced them together as best I can.

Dear Whoever Finds This Bottle:

I need your help! This letter is my only hope. I'm Erick and have been locked in my closet for two weeks. In the gray house on the corner of Oak and Pine. If you are reading this, it might already be over for me. My life as I know it anyway. I don't want to die but they say I know too much and have to make a choice between death and…something maybe worse.

They will kill me if I don't give in to what they want. You see, they want to change me into…one of them.

Sorry my writing is so messy. I'm writing in the dark. Sorry if the papers are crumply but I had to fit them inside this bottle. They gave me the soda today for my birthday, October 31. Otherwise, all I get is some water and bread or cereal. Twice a day. And I don't get bathroom breaks. Yup, bed pan city.

I'm short on time now, so here is how it all went down.

My parents were different than my friends' parents. Like, mine always encouraged me to play video games and listen to music and didn't care if I did school work.

I always got to eat pizza and burgers, whatever I wanted to. They told me how special I was. Things were just too good. Anyway, I don't know how to explain it, but I always sorta felt like they were keeping secrets from me. For one, I didn't even know what they did for jobs or how they made money.

They preferred not to be called "mom" or "dad." They liked being called by their first names: Henry and Hazel. Henry always kept all of his keys on his belt. I could hear the keys jingle-jangle whenever he was nearby. Anyway, one of the keys was red, which was strange. I'd never seen another red key and I never saw the red key open anything. Ever. But I wondered for a long time what it was for. I asked Henry once and he told me it was for good luck, like a rabbit's foot. But then he'd wink at me like he might be kidding around.

On weekends, they usually slept super late, so I'd spend the morning searching for a keyhole that might be a fit for Henry's mysterious red key. I searched every room in the house. I searched the tree house. I even looked in Jit's house. Jit is our dog. Never found anything. Sort of gave up.

Well, life— stuff happens when you least expect it. We have bookcases on both sides of the fireplace. One day I just happened to be looking for a book of stories I loved when I was really young, like when I was just a little kid. I found it right away and when I pulled it out the book next to it flopped over. I tilted it back up and noticed it seemed unusually light for such a big book, one as wide as a cereal box. The cover was dark red and the title was in creepy big white letters: Indoctrination: Inoculation of the Innocuous. Ummm, probably a book for adults, right? And then I noticed that it might not be a book at all! There was a keyhole right on a red band holding the covers closed.

I heard a noise behind me, like a gasp or whisper. I turned around expecting to see Henry or Hazel. But I was alone. My heart pounded like a drum. Just holding that book-box made me excited. Nervous too. What was inside? Did the red key open it?

It seemed important that I write the title down then I put it back *exactly* as it was. I needed a plan to get that key from Henry. I didn't have one, but I wouldn't have to wait long.

The next Saturday morning, I saw Henry's keys, the entire ring of em', resting on the hutch next to the wicker basket in the dining room. I crept upstairs; Henry and Hazel were still asleep. Now was my chance.

I swiped the keys and went to the bookshelves. I pulled out the book. The key fit. I turned it. There was a click and a pop. I carefully pulled it open.

Inside were clippings and articles about people seeing monsters. Late at night. The police dismissed some of the stories as "pranks" or "just elderly people" seeing things. But there were stories of people missing too. Disappearing. Lots of people.

One man saw a bear on two feet digging in his backyard one night. That man went missing, last seen walking his dog in Woods Park. A woman reported hearing scratching and growling noises outside her house for a bunch of nights. Days later, she was last seen playing tennis. Never heard from again.

It felt like a lightning bolt exploded in my head. I knew that somehow my parents must be wrapped up in all of this. Henry for sure and probably Hazel too. I didn't want them to catch me so I locked the book-box and put the keys back exactly where I had found them.

When I turned around, there was Henry. I swallowed a gasp. Where had he come from? We just stared at each other. The Adam's apple in his neck contracted for a few seconds and then it reappeared. My heart was drumming. I knew he knew that I knew at least some of what he knew. He looked over to his keys then back at me. Then, he latched the keys back on his belt buckle.

"What are you up to, Son?" he asked, scratching the top of his head.

"Not much." I slowly backed away.

"You sure? Somethin' you want to talk about?"

"Nope." I made it to the stairs.

"Nothin' you wanna tell me?"

"No."

I trotted up to my bedroom and closed the door. I leaned against it, slid to the floor, and tried to take long, slow breaths. Then, I made some bad choices.

First, I decided not to tell anyone what I knew. I needed to be like a spy. Then, I started staying up very late just like Henry and Hazel. I kept track of where they were. I listened to what they talked about.

And whenever I saw them I was *really* friendly. They were especially friendly to me too. They asked me way more questions than they ever used to. Especially about whom I was hanging out with at school and whom my favorite teachers to talk to were.

That was how we lived until the night of October 18. The night that they left the house at two o'clock in the morning. The night I stalked after them. I followed them through the dark night to an old stone house that looked like a mini-castle. There was even a tower! They both looked back and to the sides before creeping in a side door. They weren't the only ones. Dozens of hooded, hunched over, shadowy figures were going in.

I shivered from the cold and from what I was about to do. The door was ajar. I pulled it open. A spiral staircase led downstairs. Candles were lit along the walls. The shadows they made were spooky. Really spooky. There were strange symbols on the walls too. The noises of talking and "mingling" grew louder the further down I went.

The stairs opened to a huge room with fancy pillars, tables, and candles everywhere. There must have been a hundred people milling around. About the same number of men as women. A bunch of em' were scratching their heads just like Henry did a lot. I crouched down to stay hidden in the shadows.

A heavyset man at the front of the room commanded everyone to be silent.

"Wessrucks! Come Forth!"

Oh. My. God. These people, these FREAKS started tearing the flesh off their faces, peeling off their skin like it was old wallpaper! I expected blood and screaming until a gob of skin landed right next to me. But it wasn't skin at all! It was just Play-Dohish make-up.

And then, wigs were ripped off their heads (yes, women too) and they all clawed at their scalps like they were itchy from a thousand mosquito bites. Shirts were torn open and pelts of hair exploded out. And the sounds they made...like growls at the zoo or roars at a circus. And that wasn't the worst of it....

When some took their gloves off, I saw claws! I wished I had stayed home. I wished I could run away, but I kept watching. I had to see more. It took a minute or so for the bumps to start appearing on their faces and heads. Bumps of all different colors, bumps the size of marbles, decorating their bald heads and sprouting out from their hairy limbs. These weren't humans. These were monsters. What had the leader called them? Wessrucks? Straight from a horror movie!

Now it was time to leave. Soon as I turned to go back up the stairs, I felt the blanket go over my head and claws grasping my arms and legs. I kicked and screamed but it was no use. Their growling grew louder. I thought I was wessruck food.

Instead, I was seated and tied to a chair. When they took the blanket off, I saw dozens of wessrucks around me in a circle. I recognized Henry and Hazel. They didn't seem surprised to see me.

"Give him the serum!" one of the wessrucks shouted.

"The serum! The serum!" others joined in.

A tall and heavyset man, sorry, I meant wessruck, stepped forward. Panicking, I looked to Henry and Hazel. I was their son. Shouldn't they protect me?

"He's still too young," Hazel pleaded.

"Perhaps, but we know he knows too much," the leader replied.

"But the rule is not until he turns 13," Hazel reminded.

"He knows what we are. He knows what *you* are," the leader's eyes widened.

"The serum! The serum!" many of the other wessrucks chorused.

I begged them to let me go, and I swore up and down that I'd never say anything.

Their leader shook his head and told me that keeping their secret safe is all that matters. He said I either had to take the serum and become one of them, a wessruck, or else...

"Or else, what?" I asked.

"Or else you must die. This way, our secret will stay safe."

Then, I asked the most obvious question in the world. "But my parents are wessrucks. So I'm already one of you, aren't I?"

Some of the wessrucks laughed. It was Henry who spoke. "You can't be a full wessruck until you have been injected with the serum. You are still in the human phase. Your body is mature enough to handle the serum at 13."

"Nobody has ever been given the serum younger than 13," Hazel said.

"But it has to be this way," the wessruck leader sounded annoyed. "In two weeks' time, there will be a lunar eclipse. On this night, we will inject you, allowing you to take your wessruck form. You will occasionally hunt at night for...food. You will indulge with us as a group once a month. Your friends will no longer matter. School will no longer matter. All that matters is being a wessruck!"

"Wessrucks! Wessrucks!" Some of the beasts shouted.

I must have passed out. The next thing I remember, Henry and Hazel, looking like people again, were locking me in my room.

"You'll have to stay here the next two weeks, but then you'll be one of us!" Hazel smiled through her tears.

"I certainly hope so," Henry added. "We just don't know for sure how your body will react to the serum, but it's better than the alternative. No human can be trusted to keep our secret. Not even my son."

I tried to escape out the window the very next night and that is when they locked me in my closet.

This is my last sheet of paper. Here is the deal: I don't want to be a wessruck but I don't want to die either. I'm still holding onto hope that I might escape.

So if you are reading this note, please help me! But be careful of whom you show this letter to. If you show it to the wrong person, they will think that you "know" what you aren't supposed to "know." Remember, they only care that their secret is safe....

Sincerely,

Erick

THE CLOCK-
FIX CURSE

Hearing about dysfunctional families always makes me a little sad. Just a little…heh heh. Yet, I want to let you in on this story because it is just too delicious to keep to myself. Quite a bit spooky too!

Allow me to introduce you to Autumn. Oh no, not the season, the girl. Autumn is her given name. She doesn't feel much love for her father. But let this pose as a reminder not to judge anyone too quickly.

The insanity started when my dad walked in the house after spending all day out in his shop in the backyard. He looked really pleased with himself, even more than normal. He was carrying a decrepit looking cuckoo clock. He'd hung onto this broken "antique" forever, trying to get it to work again.

"I did it!" he exclaimed. "It took a few years but I finally got it to work!"

I didn't say anything and stayed pretty much without expression. To me, my dad was a disappointment.

"Clearly, you don't remember the morning I found this clock sitting on our front door with the strange note tied to it. And clearly, you don't have any idea how much time and energy have gone into fixing it."

Clearly I did know how much time he had spent working on that clock. So did Mom. She finally left him. The last straw was all of the time he spent working on that clock, day and night in his shop.

"Watch this!"

I did as he asked. I watched him. I watched his hands. It wasn't all that long ago that those hands handled the most delicate of instruments. He had to be so steady and precise at his old job. A job that actually mattered.

His hands were just as careful as he gently turned the delicate hour hand around until it got to 12. "*Ding!*" A little round door swung open and a bright red bird shot out. "*Cuckoo!*"

Cuckoo is right. It wasn't just the clock that was cuckoo.

"Your daddy never gives up." Dad smiled, still over the moon with himself. Sometimes I wonder if he cared more about junk than he did about people. That was mean to say, I know. I just remember how much Mom hurt and I blame a lot of it on that clock that was somehow more important than family.

"Yeah, Dad. Fixing that clock is *amazing*," I deadpanned.

"You could just pretend to be excited for once, Autumn. This is a big deal for me. I've been working to fix this clock for a long time and I finally got it working today. I thought it might get you to smile."

"I'm happy you fixed the clock, Dad. Now maybe you can return it to whoever gave it to you? Maybe it was one of your old patients and maybe they'll forgive you for those pretend cavity fillings you did? Remember those?"

I wanted to hurt him, but he seemed unfazed. He'd had the same blank cloudy stare ever since that clock arrived at our door. It was like he was in a trance.

Short-story long, that's what my dad does now. He fixes stuff. People bring him their broken junk and he spends all day—every day—out in his shop working.

He used to be a dentist. Mom was actually one of his patients and they ended up getting married. All was great until he got sued by a lot of people for filling cavities that didn't really exist. Naturally, he lost his business and it was completely embarrassing for the family. Mom stayed for a while. And me, I have to stay with Dad every other weekend as part of their divorce agreement.

Dad actually blamed all of our bad fortune on someone he called "the demon lady." Yeah, it's not a very nice name but that's what they all called her at his dental office. I guess this lady was like the worst patient ever. She'd fidget and fuss the whole time they cleaned her teeth. They gave her music to try to relax her but she still went crabapple on them. I remember hearing about her when I was little; I saw her once too. One of her front teeth was missing and she had strange gray hair with a thick gold streak in the front. Reddish eyes. Apparently, Dad suggested many times that she go to a different dentist but she always declined. On one visit, she asked for Dad to give her a new front tooth. Oh wait, I remember her name! Lizbeth Lilith. Anyway, she insisted that they give her a gold tooth. Dad said she already had the tooth and was wearing it on a necklace: EEW!

Dad said she was responsible for spreading all of the lies about his practice, forcing it to close down. She accused him of taking advantage of people by filling cavities that weren't real. People believed her.

I made something to eat before locking myself in my tiny bedroom where I spent the night playing on my phone. The next morning, Dad's cheerfulness had returned as if my insulting him yesterday had never happened.

"Wake up, Autumn! We've got ourselves a busy mornin'!"

I sat up, pointed a finger at him, and raised my voice. "I'll stay in bed thanks. You don't need me to go get donuts with you. You don't need me to sit in the car while it runs through the car wash. And, lastly, you don't need me to go to the home goods store to walk down every single aisle. You do the same things every time I am here!"

Dad was completely unfazed by my spitefulness. "Nope! Halloween is right around the corner and we need to pick up a few pumpkins, don't you think? Thought we might carve one soon."

Too much energy and excitement for me in the morning. So, I turned over in bed and did my best *I'm still asleep* impression.

"I can't accept no for an answer. We've gotta hurry and get to the pumpkin patch so we get firstees!"

I played dead. Wait, did he say pumpkin patch? It'd been years since I'd been to one of those. Suddenly, I was certain I knew the *real* reason he wanted to go to a pumpkin patch. And it all comes back to fixing that clock. Whoever left that clock at our door left a note with instructions for what to do after fixing the clock. Something about finding a green...no, a blue pumpkin! So, my dad wanted me to go with him on his treasure hunt. What a freak. And he used to say that old demon lady should be in a loony bin.

I heard Dad call to me from downstairs. "Fine, be that way. I went and got those sausage-cheese biscuits you love for breakfast. I guess if you don't want them, I'll have to wolf em' down!"

My weakness. Was. A. Good. Breakfast. I got out of bed and went downstairs. I finished eating and I knew there was a price to pay; I'd have to spend the rest of the morning with him. But really, I was getting old for pumpkin patches. I couldn't wait 'til Mom picked me up later that afternoon.

At the pumpkin patch, we were the first ones there, just like Dad wanted. He tried to give me a high-five but I kept my head and hand down. He told me I could pick out any pumpkin I wanted and if I smiled for him, I could pick two.

I went off, wandering the patch on my own. I just wanted to kill some time. I had no intention of picking any pumpkins. I actually sat down on the ground and people watched for a while.

"CHA-CHA-CHING!"

I recognized my dad's yell even though he was half of a football field away. I watched him sprinting toward the cashiers. His arms were out in front of him like he was carrying the Olympic torch.

I was embarrassed to be standing next to him at the cashier. His hands were shaking as he thumbed through his wallet for cash. He was buying a blue pumpkin. Yes, blue. Like somewhere between the color of the sky and a blue ribbon.

"I just knew I'd find one Autumn! I knew it! Just like that note said. Once I fixed the clock I'd find a blue pumpkin." Dad looked at me through eyes that seemed to be out of focus. Then he recited the lines from the note, word for word:

When a clock long broken, can suddenly tick
And a bizarre blue pumpkin, is there to pick
And a doll in a window, pleads with forlorn eyes
'Neath orange moon and night sky, the devil shall rise

The woman behind the table chuckled, and I hid in the car.

At home, Dad put the blue pumpkin on the piano bench minutes before Mom arrived. I couldn't wait to get back to my full-time home.

For the next two weeks, I kept healthy and positive thoughts. In other words, I hardly thought about my dad and his growing mental illness. But the time passed fast and on the night before Halloween, I was back at Dad's. This would be our first Halloween alone together. I vowed not to go trick-or-treating with him.

But instead of cracking jokes as usual, he just kept repeating the lines from the strange note over and over.

When a clock long broken, can suddenly tick
And a bizarre blue pumpkin, is there to pick
And a doll in a window, pleads with forlorn eyes
'Neath orange moon and night sky, the devil shall rise

Apparently he'd been trying to find that doll for two weeks.

"I know I've seen a doll in a window somewhere, Autumn," Dad said, eyes glazed over, pacing the living room in circles. "I know it. I know it. It's the last piece of the riddle." He stopped. "Hey, I have an idea! Let's go get some pizza!"

Usually, he fried potatoes on Saturday, which I actually liked since he'd burn them a little to bring out their flavor. It was obvious he had other things on his mind and that it wasn't really pizza he wanted. So, off I went on his little treasure hunt.

We drove through the old part of town and in front of practically every building with a light on, Dad slammed on the brakes thinking he might see a doll. The whiplash soured my appetite and I only ate a couple slices. He didn't seem to notice or care.

Just before we finally turned into the driveway, Dad slammed the breaks. Again. "I just had a thought! There's a doll in Janestown. It's on the top floor of a house. In a window. Can't believe I just thought of it. I'll be right back!"

Before I closed the car door I said, "You've lost it, Dad. When you go to jail for robbery, don't call me or Mom."

I sat inside and played on my phone for a while. Out the window between the branches of an old elm tree, I saw the full moon rising. It was as orange as a pumpkin. Well, a normal pumpkin, not the blue one sitting on the piano bench right over…with smoke coming out of the top of its stem? A sudden chill swept down my back and my heart started pounding. I squinted hard. I walked closer. A cloud of wispy smoke was definitely rising for the stem of the blue pumpkin. Then the smoke gathered and formed a cloud. It was like watching a genie coming forth from a bottle. Except, well, it was coming out of the stem of a blue pumpkin. I began to see the makings of a figure inside the cloud. A person?

"No way," I whispered. I had only seen her once before but I recognized that face. The demon lady from Dad's dental office! Her eyes were ferociously red, like fireballs, and I'd never forget that gold streak of hair in her thick gray mane. She knew the second I recognized her. She smiled, and I saw that golden tooth.

A halo of light now surrounded her, and I could see red bumps all over her skin. Her eyes never once left mine. I screamed as she descended to the floor.

She let out something between a shriek and a howl, stinging my eardrums. I started to run but felt something cold wrap around my leg. I was able to jerk free but with every step I felt something icy cold close behind.

In back of me, Lizbeth Lilith was howling like a rabid wolf. I lunged forward, my body sliding underneath the dining room table to the other side. When I stood up, Lizbeth and I were face-to-face. Sweat was pouring down my forehead and I was panting.

Her unnaturally long fingernails ripped into the table, making saw-like sounds as they dug into the wood. When Lizbeth leapt at me, I ducked, barely missing getting clawed.

I sprinted around the table and into the foyer. I needed to get outside. That's when I felt a sharp sting in my back. She got me! I screamed so loud. She grabbed my neck with her hands. I flipped over and kicked at her but she was way too strong. Her red eyes bulged. I began to fade.

Next thing I know, someone pulled her off of me. Dad!

I was still working to breathe and couldn't sit up, but I heard the two of them struggling.

"NOOOOO!" Lizbeth yelled.

And then, nothing. Silence until I felt my dad's arms around me and heard his sobs.

"The clock. She must have cursed it. But she wanted to hurt me. Not you. Oh, Autumn, how could I have let this happen?"

Through his tears I could see his eyes looked normal again. No more trance. And no more Lizbeth. On the floor next to him was a doll dressed in a beautiful white dress with sad green eyes. The final ingredient. Lizbeth must have been...summoned once he had it in his possession.

"So you're saying that this whole thing with you fixing the clock, finding the blue pumpkin and the doll...that it was all part of a curse?"

"And somehow we broke it. Perhaps it had something to do with this," Dad said, holding up the golden tooth stuck between a set of pliers. "I felt like a dentist again," Dad smirked.

The scene was so absurd, I giggled. Between the shock and fear and relief, the two of us started laughing like idiots. I forgot to ask where the pliers came from.

I finally settled down. "So this is over?"

"How about some fried potatoes?" Dad smiled.

After our second dinner, I went to bed. I remembered the wound Lizbeth had inflicted on my back. I had forgotten to tend to it. I went to clean it. She got me pretty good. I don't know why, but I went downstairs and found that golden tooth my dad had thrown in the garbage. I put it in my pocket.

MY MOM, THE
UNDERTAKER

I still have a hard time accepting this poor soul's story. But it's all true, as I confirmed the details with other sources. Perhaps you might be tempted to find his story funny, if you have a dark sense of humor. Imagine one day if you went outside of your house and you found a human skull sticking out of the grass in the front yard. What would you think? What would you do? Who would you tell? Well, before I get too far into the story let me tell it to you just as it was told to me, straight from the mouth of Clive Mortell, an 11-year-old boy with a most unusual situation.

My mom was an undertaker. Yeah, you heard right. My mother, an *undertaker*. Oh, wait. I'm sorry. "Undertaker" probably isn't considered a proper title anymore. Mortician? Nope! "Mortician" is also inappropriate. "Funeral Director" is most comfortable for people to say. But Mom had "Undertaker" on her business card because she felt responsible for *taking* the dead *under*ground and guiding their souls into the beyond. To her, funeral directors handle the business and undertakers are the spiritual guides.

Yeah, so burying the dead was a very personal thing for my mom. She took care of absolutely everything, from driving to get the dead bodies to storing them until they were claimed (sometimes this took a while), and prepping them for burial or cremation.

We lived in a small logging town with only a few thousand people. There weren't a lot of amenities, so our house doubled as the town's funeral home. I know, right? Who does that? Well, we did. Just me and my mom. In our house, the bedrooms were upstairs; the kitchen, dining, and family rooms were part of the main floor where there was also a room for the business side— you know like, viewings, funerals, and all of that.

Lastly, there was the basement where Mom worked at night. Oh, and yeah, we drove a hearse! I know you were wondering.

So about our basement. Mom made me promise a long time ago that I never go down there. That was her domain and I was forbidden. She called it her "other" family room. That's all she ever asked of me, but I didn't really like it. I mean, we lived alone, just the two of us, and sometimes it seemed like she would rather be down there with the dead people than with me.

Yeah, I get that you might think it's strange to live in a funeral home with dead bodies in the basement all the time. But think of the stuff I got to experience. I'm pretty sure I saw ghosts at night; I know I heard them, like when they'd bang on my walls or walk down the hall outside my room. Those were the traumatized ghosts that Mom said were stuck here like in limbo between worlds. I don't want to scare you but some of the more angry ghosts would shake my bed while I tried to sleep. And I already mentioned the hearse. Kinda cool, huh?

I would hear my mom whispering late at night to her "other" family. She said it's all part of guiding the dead—especially the lost souls and ghosts still hanging around—safely on their way. She helped them get to where they needed to go, or something.

Sometimes after a funeral, if a dead body was really heavy, Mom would ask for my help carrying it outside— usually in a coffin, of course—so she could bury it. Did I mention that we lived next door to the cemetery? I'm not kidding.

One week, Mom seemed to be getting busier with work. I'd never seen her working so much or so hard. Every single night we had dead visitors—bodies. There were all kinds of living people coming and going too.

I admit, I was jealous. But it sounds so stupid to be jealous of dead people, even if she considered them her "other family." Part of me was fuming mad. But another part of me wanted to see if there was something I could do to help her. So, I made up my mind. I decided to break the one promise that I ever made her. When I got home from track practice and noticed she was sleeping, I opened the door to the basement. Yeah, I was headed to the "other family" rooms.

I broke into a cold sweat walking down those hard concrete steps. I was shaking a little too. What would I find? What was *really* down here? What wasn't I supposed to see?

After more than 50 steps, my foot finally tapped the floor at the bottom. It didn't take long to smell one of the reasons why Mom didn't want me down here. The rancid odors got my eyes watering and my stomach turning. I had to hold my nose.

It was totally dark other than the little beam of light streaming in from upstairs, which didn't help much. I felt along the clammy walls to find a light switch. Then I started opening doors. There were a couple of big closets full of sharp tools and containers. There was also a room with empty coffins and urns. I knew what all that stuff was for. I heard Mom explain it many times. But when I opened the room with the bodies, the cold that drifted out felt like being outside in winter. I sensed that *this* is where I really wasn't supposed to be.

I felt a little like an ice cube: really cold. I was only wearing a t-shirt, shorts, my necklace, and my ball cap. A machine in the wall hummed so loudly I couldn't hear my footsteps or the flick of the light switch. The smell was way worse than before. I did my best not to puke. Imagine putting your face in a garbage can full of rotten eggs covered up by medicine. Yeah, that's kind of how I thought it smelled.

I noticed some tools carefully placed on a long table in the middle of the room. The entire back wall was lined with drawer handles. But my attention was completely drawn to two tables covered by sheets. Something was under those sheets. Was that...were these new members of Mom's other family? I peeked under one of the sheets. I mean, I made it this far and I guess I wanted to make sure. The corpse was super pale. His eyes had been sewn closed and there were cotton balls stuffed in his nose.

The dead body was naked and was hairy; I saw a beard. I poked it quick and it felt slippery, brittle and stiff like the clay bowl I made in art class. Yuck. He was missing a hand too. Maybe *this* was that local lumberjack who chainsawed off his hand last week? I threw the sheet back over him.

I saw a hand draped over the side of the table under the other sheet. It had really long gray fingernails. I didn't want to get close to it. What if that hand like moved or something and grabbed me?

My attention was drawn to some…lava lamps, or something that looked a lot like them. There were two: one was red and the other was blue and there were bubbles inside that were moving and glowing. They were on the ends of a long table covered with a fancy looking sheet. Between the lamps was a massive book that looked heavier than the table. This must be the "spiritual" part of what Mom did, what she didn't want me to know about. Nor did I want to. I had seen enough. Actually, I had seen too much.

My stomach had had enough too. I quickly understood that I wasn't well suited to help Mom with anything down here. I wondered if I'd see her differently now. I closed the door and headed for the stairs when I heard her footsteps. She was ringing a bell and reciting something, prayers maybe? She said it cleaned the air of bad spirits and would only do it before...working.

I couldn't let her find me down here! Remember, she only ever asked me for one thing: to stay out of the basement. *Her* basement. And I had now officially broken that promise.

I didn't have time to sneak into the coffin room. The only way to go was back into *that* room. I remembered seeing some drawers on the back wall. In the dark, I pulled the handle of one and a long metal tray rolled out. My nose hit something rubbery, which I think—I hope—was just the foot of a cadaver. I quickly but quietly pushed it shut. I pulled handles until I found an empty drawer. I quietly rolled onto the tray, lay flat on my back, and—using my hands—I pushed on the metal ceiling until the tray rolled backward on its own. Then I heard a click.

I tried not to move, not to breathe. Even if I wanted to fidget, it wasn't possible. Let's just say I had no wiggle-room. Imagine being in a top bunk with your nose touching the ceiling. It was pitch-black in there. No light whatsoever. But it seemed to be a good hiding place. Mom must have come in the room since I could hear her muffled chanting and she hadn't found me.

I was getting cold. I felt like I was inside of a refrigerator. It didn't take long before my teeth started to jitter, then my body started to shiver. I couldn't help it. I thought for sure I was making enough noise and Mom would hear me. I kept waiting for the little chamber door to open and for the look of disappointment when she busted me. But it didn't happen.

Soon my shivering turned into uncontrollable shaking, like I was riding in the back of a big truck driving over speed bumps. Mom must have gone back upstairs or for sure she would have heard me.

I realized I was stuck in this tiny space with no way out. I slammed my feet against the wall but I realized that click I heard earlier meant I was locked in. My breathing was heavy. Why was it so hard to breathe? I was gasping for air. I couldn't get enough into my lungs. Could I actually run out of oxygen in here?

The thought of suffocating jolted me like lightning. I tried to sit up but my forehead slammed into the metal ceiling. I tried to shift myself around so that I could try to open the door with my hands but there wasn't any room. I had gone in head first. So, I kicked harder and harder. And I shouted. I shouted for Mom! I'd give anything for her to open the door and save me. She could ground me for life. I kicked with all my might. I made choking noises as I tried to suck every last bit of air out of the darkness. One last kick was all I had left in me. I remember feeling pain inside my chest and then everything went dark.

The next thing I remember is feeling like I was dreaming. I saw the red and blue lava lamps and my mom was reading from that big book. But she was crying too. Really hard. Her hands were moving in circles around me. I wanted to tell her I was sorry but my mouth didn't work. I watched as she shook her head back and forth. Then she put her hands over her face. She had failed at whatever she was trying to do and the lava lights went out.

In the mirror on the side of our hearse, there was no reflection of me. I was dead. I had become a lost soul. I watched from a distance as they buried my coffin into the ground. I saw some of my friends and of course my mom was there. I remember the day really well. The sun was out and the autumn wind made all of the colorful leaves dance about. My mom was sobbing.

I couldn't stand seeing all of the hurt I had caused my mom and I didn't want to stay around. I felt so ashamed. Not really knowing what to do as a ghost, I just wandered. Time truly has no meaning when you're dead but I must have wandered for a really long time. One day, I decided to go back home and see if there was a way that I could let Mom know how sorry I felt. I also wanted her to forgive me for breaking the promise.

When I got there, the house was gone and there were bulldozers everywhere. Even the cemetery had been left to rot. I was going to leave (and never return) when I saw something really unusual looking popping up from the grass. At first glance I thought it was a rock, but then I saw the empty eye sockets. It was a skull. A human skull. Also sticking out of the ground was a tiny silver bird, which I recognized as part of my necklace. It must have been buried with me. I knew the skull was...mine.

I needed to find someone like my mom with that special gift to help stranded ghosts like me. I decided my best bet was to go house-to-house and maybe thump on some walls, or make other noises...surely someone is out there who can help me?

THE NIGHTMIRROR

There is a small town, not far from where you live, where Halloween is never celebrated. EVER. October 31 is *mostly* just another day. I say mostly because there is a dark secret about Halloween of which only adults are aware.

In this town, on October 31, the grocery stores get unusually busy and close early. In this town, on October 31, people finish their errands quickly in order to get home before the sun goes down. Everyone leaves the lights on all night. Oh, and one last thing: many people cover their windows and *everyone* covers all the mirrors.

Moving to a new house in a new town can be exciting but definitely has its drawbacks, particularly leaving old friends behind. Not to mention the drudgery of packing and unpacking.

Aiden wiped his sweaty forehead on his shoulder as he lifted another box out of the rented truck. He was moving in with his mother, Jenny, full-time. This was the house she grew up in, Grandma and Grandpa's old house. Aiden already missed his friends but was glad his cousin Charlie had flown in from the big city.

After a day of heavy lifting and tearing open more boxes than they thought possible, the three of them sat down to dinner, ravenous.

"So what do you guys have planned for the evening?" Jenny asked. "I made sure to get the Xbox connected for you."

"Trick-or-treating!" Charlie shouted through a mouth full of mashed potatoes.

Aiden, also with a mouthful of food, grunted in agreement.

Jenny's face turned pale and she dropped her fork on her plate. "Aiden, we discussed that things are different here in this town. October 31 is just a normal night, like any other. You're not in your dad's town anymore."

"Aw come on! Dad even bought me a costume. Why are you acting so weird about it, Mom? What's the big deal?"

"*My mom* says she wants me to bring her some candy, even if it's from the store," Charlie chimed in.

Jenny's hands shook as she blotted her forehead with her napkin. "I'm sorry but you and Char-bar are going to have to find something else to do. I want you safe inside tonight."

Back in Aiden's room, Charlie went into the closet and walked out minutes later dressed as an astronaut, complete with space helmet. "Ready for warp speed, Captain Aiden? Let's go get us some candy!"

Aiden frowned. "I don't know, Char. I've never seen my mom so freaked out," he mumbled.

They heard Jenny's phone ring downstairs.

"She's usually on the phone for a long time though," Aiden said smiling at Charlie.

"The timing couldn't be more perfect. It's a sign from the gods! We'll sneak out for a bit and she'll never know," Charlie said clapping his hands together and touching one of the buttons on his costume. "Beam us out, Aiden!"

Aiden laughed and quickly transformed into a golfer complete with knickers, long socks, flat hat, and golf club. He put a small flashlight in a pocket and led his cousin down the back stairs and into the night.

They raced together down the sidewalk looking for a house to visit. Aiden thought it was odd to not see any orange lights or spooky decorations anywhere. There weren't any jack-o'-lanterns either. Aiden slowed to a walk and peered down the street in both directions: not a single car, person, or trick-or-treater.

"Char? Maybe we should go home. This all feels wrong to me," Aiden said. "We're all alone out here."

Charlie held up his puffy gloves in front of Aiden's face. "NO FUN ALERT! NO FUN! NO FUN!" Charlie said opening and closing his hands and eyes in tandem with the words.

"Fine. We'll try another block," Aiden consented remembering it was Charlie who helped him move all day. But soon it became crystal clear nobody was celebrating Halloween.

"All right. I'm really creeped out. Let's go home and play vid…" Aiden's voice trailed off when he didn't see his cousin behind him. By the time Aiden found Charlie, it was too late.

"Trick-or-treat!" Charlie shouted thumping on someone's front door. No one answered but Aiden saw a man suspiciously peek out from behind the curtains.

Charlie sprinted to the front door of another house. When Aiden caught up to him, Charlie was rudely buzzing the doorbell.

DING! DING! DING! DING! DING!

Just like the last house, nobody came to the door. An elderly man nervously pulled aside the curtains. The man had a large shotgun at his side!

"Charlie, we're going home. Dude has a gun! My mom was right. Something really strange is going on." Aiden felt a chilly sweat inside the brim of his flat hat.

Though Aiden didn't care for the *'quit being such a wimp'* look Charlie gave him, he was thankful his cousin was at least following him down the sidewalk.

They were a block from home when Charlie turned to Aiden and beamed him in the face with his laser-gun. Bright red light blasted Aiden's eyes. Charlie changed the color of the light to green and then to blue. Momentarily blinded, Aiden tripped and fell.

Aiden blinked and blinked until his vision returned. Charlie was nowhere to be seen. He shouted for his cousin but got no reply.

A hazy blue light appeared in the attic of an old house up ahead. It flashed off for a second but quickly came back on. It was surely Charlie and his obnoxious laser-gun. But how could he be so stupid as to wander into a stranger's home? Unlike the rest of the well-lit neighborhood, this house was completely dark. Had Charlie lost his mind?

Aiden shouted for his cousin to come outside. The house had a cracked 'For Sale' sign dangling awkwardly from a post in the front yard. The windows were boarded. A huge dead oak tree leaned dangerously over the roof, its branches groaning in the wind. Aiden couldn't return home without Charlie. He knew he had to go inside and retrieve his naughty cousin.

The screen door was missing its screen and was light as a feather to pull open. As Aiden was reaching for the solid wood front door, it mysteriously swung open on its own. Charlie must not have closed it. Dust from the floor swirled into the air making Aiden cough. Still no sign of Charlie.

Switching on his flashlight, Aiden walked up the dust-covered stairs. He was doing his best to be quiet. Was it possible that someone could actually be here? What if someone caught them?

At the top of the steps, there was still no sign of Charlie but the scuttle door to the attic was open and the ladder stairs down. Aiden wondered if Charlie was up there at all. What would he find?

Once in the attic, Aiden received both good and bad news. Fortunately, he found the source of the blue light he saw from the street. It was coming from a huge, partially covered mirror on the floor leaning against the wall. The light of the full moon was hitting the exposed bottom corner of the mirror creating the unusual glow. That was the good news. Unfortunately, there was no sign of Charlie, which meant Aiden was all alone in the attic of an abandoned house.

"HEY YOU!"

Aiden's heart flew into his throat. The flashlight fell from his hand and instinctively, he grasped the golf club like a weapon. He spun around and found himself face-to-face with a spaceman. Charlie.

"How the heck did you…oh, never mind. Let's get out of here!" Aiden was an emotional milkshake of relief, anger, and terror.

"I was just playing around. I hid behind a tree and you walked right by, so I followed you up here." Charlie replied, a bit too casually for his cousin.

"We're going. Now!" Aiden reached for Charlie's arm to pull him toward the ladder but Charlie darted away.

"Charlie, we *have* to get out of here. This isn't our house! Where did you go now?" Aiden grabbed his flashlight but other than a rocking chair, a broken book case, and the covered mirror, the attic appeared empty.

Looking closer, Aiden noticed one of Charlie's space boots sticking out beneath the sheet covering the mirror. Aiden knelt down and with both hands and tugged on his cousin's leg. "Come on!"

"Wait, look at this!" Charlie pulled the sheet off the mirror and rubbed the glass with his thumb. "Hand prints. On the *inside* of the glass!"

The mirror now lit up the attic with its eerie blue glow.

Aiden turned toward the attic door in the floor. "That's it, Charlie. I'm going home and leaving you here. We're in deep troub..."

CHARRRRRLIEEEEE...

It was a whisper. Not a man or woman's whisper... something else.

"Woah!" Charlie fell backward.

HEEEELLLLLLLP ME, CHARRRRRLIEEEEEE...

The whisper was clearer. The voice sounded closer now too.

"How can I help you? Are you trapped in there?" Charlie shouted tapping on the glass like it was a fish tank at the pet store.

"Charlie, something really strange is going on AND we're not supposed to be here," Aiden pleaded with his cousin.

HANNNNNDDDSSSSSS, CHARRRRRLLIEEEEEE

The wispy voice sounded like it was standing right next to Charlie. It sounded tired and weary, yet somehow... threatening. Charlie focused only on the mirror, entranced.

YOUR HANNNNNDDDSSSSSS, CHARRRRRLLIEEEEEE... HURRYYYY

Charlie held up his gloved hands and slowly moved them toward the prints on the mirror.

"No! Charlie! Don't do it!" Aiden warned, running toward his cousin, golf club at the ready to smash the mirror. But he was too late. The instant Charlie touched the mirror, a pair of ghastly hands appeared from the other side and grabbed Charlie's wrists, hoisting him through the mirror without any of the glass breaking.

Aiden heard screams and the sounds of a struggle. He shouted for his cousin until his was the only voice. It was quiet again.

If he smashed the mirror, would his cousin reappear safe and sound? Or, what if breaking the mirror made it impossible for Charlie to return, trapping him inside forever?

So Aiden ran home, as fast as he could. He burst inside and told his mom what had happened. Jenny slumped onto the couch and pulled Aiden into a hug.

"Mom, stop. We have to go back and get Charlie out of there!"

"We do have to go back, Aiden…to cover that mirror. The Nightmirror Spirit uses mirrors, sometimes even windows, as portals into the living world. He steals kids that way."

Aiden watched Jenny trying to be strong, fighting back tears.

"This evil spirit mostly uses the mirrors to snatch people, especially children, and seal them forever in its dark spirit world. The story is that it's actually the ghost of a very troubled boy who was teased relentlessly about how he looked. He grew up hating mirrors. Instead of moving on after dying, he stayed behind, tormenting the town for revenge. And he does so only on Halloween Night."

Aiden looked deeply into her eyes. "Mom, we still have to try."

"Aiden, I need you to understand that Charlie isn't coming back."

When they got to the rundown house, Aiden led his mom into the attic. The moon was higher in the sky and the last bit of moonlight lit the attic in a dull, hazy shade of blue.

Aiden shined his flashlight into the mirror. The hand prints were still there. Two sets of them now. Aiden heard a whisper.

"Did you hear that? I think it was Charlie. He must have seen my light!"

Jenny shook her head side to side. "Charlie is gone! Nobody has ever come back once they've been pulled through to the other side." She picked the dark sheet up off the floor and walked toward the mirror.

AIIIDDDEEENNNNNN, GIVE ME YOUR HANNNNDS

"I heard him, Mom! He needs my help!"

"For the good of the town, Aiden. The mirror must be covered. Charlie is gone."

"No! Maybe if Charlie sees my hands he can grab them and..."

Aiden suddenly felt icy cold hands grab his own. Jenny screamed behind him as Aiden flew face first into the mirror. Aiden braced for pain but there was none. But he felt really cold as his body went through.

And just like that, he was on the other side. The mirror was behind him and he could see Jenny with her hands cupped around her eyes. He watched her mouth open and close. She was shouting his name. *Aiden! Aiden!* He watched her lips move but he couldn't hear her.

Like a curtain dropping at the end of a play, the Nightmirror Spirit appeared in front of the mirror, blocking Aiden from seeing his mom. Aiden gasped and fell on the ground. It drifted toward him like a ghost: sunken face, skeletal teeth, a smattering of white hair, and tattered rags that had been clothes long ago. The image would haunt his thoughts for as long as he lived.

Aiden jumped to his feet and pulled out his golf club. But the Nightmirror Spirit had disappeared just as quickly as it had appeared. Aiden used his club to poke into the darkness around him. Suddenly, a voice.

"Don't hit me!"

Aiden recognized the voice instantly but it was too dark to see. The only light was coming from the other side of the mirror.

"Charlie!"

"I'm right behind you," Charlie said grabbing his cousin's hand.

Aiden spun about. "Why did you drag me in here? I was trying to help get *you* out of here."

"I didn't bring you here! That ghost did. It made itself sound like me to trick you," Charlie said. "It's pure evil, Aiden. *Pure* evil. It told me…"

"Talk later dude, we gotta get out of here," Aiden said turning back toward the mirror.

"No!" Aiden and Charlie shouted at the same time.

On the other side of the mirror, Aiden and Charlie watched Jenny pick the sheet up off the floor and begin to cover the mirror. She was sobbing.

The cousins sprinted toward the mirror, shouting and waving their arms in hopes of stopping Jenny from doing what she believed she had to do. And then, the mirror was covered and the boys stood together in absolute darkness.

Aiden couldn't believe Jenny had given up on them. His heart sank.

For the good of the town, Aiden thought.

Aiden couldn't believe how dark it got. Then he saw a red spot in the distance. No, a pair of spots. Then two

more. *Eyes,* Aiden realized. In the distance, he heard tor-
turous screams, bellows, barking, and shrieks from...
*things...*lurking in the dark.

"What is this place," Aiden asked his cousin. "Who else
is here?"

"He called it his nightmare world. He said we'd soon
turn into lost spirits like them and live here forever,"
Charlie said.

"Then we need to get out of here," Aiden said. "We
need to find an uncovered mirror somehow. Somewhere. "

Charlie flicked on his space light. "The spirits don't
like the light now that they're...permanent residents here.
They'll stay away from us as long as we keep the light on."

Aiden looked at Charlie. "But what happens when the
batteries die?"

MAGGIE AND
MAGLICH

Maggie Lichtenstein was a normal eight-year-old girl but what became of her, I'm sorry to say, is tragic. And terrible.

First, a bit about Maggie; she had a lot of friends, enjoyed TV and video games, sports, and even liked school (except art class). But more than anything, she loved to eat desserts. In particular, she loved pumpkin pie.

Maggie loved pumpkin pie so much that sometimes she would bury a frozen Mrs. Johnson pie deep into the grocery cart so her mom wouldn't see. And sometimes, she'd sneak out of her bed late at night to steal a piece from the fridge.

Now, this was all fine and dandy until the morning that Maggie awoke very sick. She was confined to her bed with tummy aches, dizziness, and that hot-cold-hot-cold feeling you get when your body is working extremely hard to fight a malady.

Sadly, the illness caused her to miss an inordinate amount of school. Her principal was very strict about attendance and it was decided that she would have to repeat the second grade. This, unfortunately, led to her being teased and taunted by kids that used to be her friends.

For months, doctors and scientists poked, prodded, and tested Maggie to try and diagnose her illness. They developed a theory that consuming large amounts of beta-carotene, a major ingredient in pumpkins, led to her serious allergic reactions. Maggie decided she hated her symptoms more than she loved the taste of pumpkin pie. She vowed to never eat it again.

As Maggie got older, she found her distaste for all-things-pumpkin growing. She would even excuse herself if a pumpkin pie was simply placed on the dinner table. In fourth grade, Maggie's art teacher described her painting of frowny-faced pumpkins as "crazy." In junior high, she earned the nickname "Mental Maggie" after giving a speech about the dangers of pumpkin overdose.

In high school, Maggie was sent to the principal's office for tearing Halloween decorations of pumpkins off the walls. "What's the matter with you?" her principal asked. "Are you insane?"

Soon, all it took was the sight of something orange, a road construction cone or an autumn leaf, to trigger an unhappy stomach—or worse.

One October, an all-grown-up Maggie decided to try a different kind of doctor in the hope of finding a cure. Maggie told her everything but for a while the doctor said nothing. She just sat and stared, making Maggie very uncomfortable.

"Maggie, people have called you crazy. Insane. Even psycho."

Each word stung. The doctor continued, a gleam in her eye. "Well, I don't agree." Maggie couldn't tell if the doctor was being honest or...

"You know Maggie, some people have been able to achieve relief by directly confronting their issues. " The doctor had a gentle smile, but Maggie wondered if it was genuine.

"Sometimes if you're scared of close quarters, you need to ride an elevator. If you are scared of heights, start by climbing a few rungs on a ladder. You know, I actually hate bees and…"

Wait, Maggie wondered. *Did the doctor just make fun of me? Is she mocking me? She is supposed to help me.*

Wary but with no other options, Maggie decided to try the doctor's advice. Late that night, she left home with a flashlight and headed to the nearest pumpkin patch. She opened the gate and walked to the middle of the patch surrounded by dozens and dozens of pumpkins. Her insides began to churn. An ache erupted in her temple.

I must fight this!

Suddenly, she heard a tiny voice. Just a whisper really. The sound a mouse might make if it could talk. Soon, one whisper became many.

"Maggie…Maggie. You're weak. You're stupid. You fear us. We are better than you."

Maggie looked around. The voices could only be coming from one place. *Godforsaken pumpkins! They're taunting me.*

Maggie's tummy started to do roller coasters and her head exploded.

Hold on a little longer, Maggie, she told herself. *Doctor said I must confront my fears. Then I will be cured.*

Not strong enough to hold it back, she let the past come rushing back, roaring through her head like a freight train: the illness, missing school, repeating second grade, the teasing from the kids, teachers, and even her doctor.

Maggie shrieked a battle cry as she slammed her foot down on the pumpkin closest to her. A large piece broke off the side. Electric tingles surged through her body and Maggie felt alive for the first time in years. *Really* alive. Even better, she felt in control. Everything started to make sense. She felt as though she had been working on a 1,000,000 piece jigsaw puzzle. And, this was the last piece.

I see now! Everything bad that happened to me was because of the pumpkins! Even now, they tease and laugh at me! And what did I ever do other than love pumpkin pies? Pumpkins ruined my life...

Her head was finally, mercifully quiet. Still. But not a second later, the whispers returned.

"You're crazy Mental-Maggie. If anyone sees you they'll know you're insane."

Headlights from a passing car brought her out of her reverie. Stumbling past vines and pumpkins, Maggie stormed out of the patch. But she had a plan. She would get *them* later. She would get *all* of *them*.

Maggie's mind bubbled with ideas on her way home. She felt strong for the first time since before her illness all those years ago. She realized that in order to be normal again, she needed to get rid of—no, annihilate—all of the pumpkins in town. To do that, she would have to become invisible. If anyone saw her, they'd stop her. They wouldn't understand her plight.

The next afternoon, Maggie sewed herself a long, dark hooded robe. At the shoe repair, she had the cobbler fashion her boots with heavy steel toes and heels. Finally, she found a walking stick in her backyard to keep her steady while roaming through various patches in the dark.

Maggie studied herself in the mirror. What she usually saw was someone weak, frail, and fragile. Someone easy to take advantage of. Highly sensitive. But today, she saw a fiercely independent and strong woman. A woman in control. Finally. After a lifetime of suffering.

Maggie crawled into bed. She fell asleep and dreamt she met a person wearing a dark robe exactly like the one she made. When the woman pulled the hood aside. Maggie was shocked to see herself. "*Hello, sister. Maggie is no longer. You are Maglich now.*"

She awoke the next morning feeling like she now possessed the strength of two.

That night, the air was chilly but her robe kept her warm as she walked. At the patch entrance, she flung the gate open and pointed her flashlight out at the sea of pumpkins. She heard them whispering. They knew who she was. They knew why she was there.

The first pumpkin split easily beneath the power of her steel boot. The next few hours were sheer bliss, crunching row after row of pumpkins, leaving an orange mess in her wake. With each pumpkin she killed, the whispers faded. When she had cleared the entire patch of the orange beasts, she walked home peacefully. Her mind was quiet. The sun was just about to rise. She slept all day.

When the sun set that evening, she visited the only other pumpkin patch for many miles and spent the entire night stomping. She was sure she had destroyed them all. But as she was changing out her robe back at home, she heard a single, small whisper in her head. *"You forgot about me. I'm still alive."*

There must be at least one more pumpkin still out there. Her face reddened and her nostrils flared. *Maglich will need help to get rid of them. Maglich can't do it alone. But Maglich still did good.*

Almost a full year went by. Maglich had been busy planning. When the following October came around, Maglich donned her robe, staff, and boots and entered a pumpkin patch as the sun went down. But this time, instead of destroying them all like last year, she saved two. She drew out a long knife and severed their stems with such hostility that she nearly chopped off her own a finger. Then, she dropped them into a dark bag and brought them home.

"Vile creatures!" Maglich screamed. Touching them made her feel woozy. The smell of them nearly made her pass out. But she had a job to do.

Clutching the knife with both hands raised high over her head, she plunged the knife in and out of the two pumpkins, to get to their pulpy centers.

We're gonna make some pumpkin pie!

After pulling the pies from the oven, she sprinkled some poison powder atop each one.

Not enough to kill. Just enough to make very, very ill!

The next morning, she carefully wrapped the pies and put on a warm smile. She hand delivered a pie to the rest home, a church, the local food shelter, and an orphanage.

It feels so nice to feed those in need.

At the grocery store, she sprinkled poison powder on each of the pumpkin pies in the bakery. She was careful not to be seen and kept her back turned when a shopper walked by.

Don't mind me. Just inspecting the pies for…freshness.

Within the week, dozens of people were reported ill. Many were so sick they had to go the hospital. A special medical staff was dispatched to the rest home and the orphanage. Once the story hit the news, people started to panic. The sickness was quickly traced back to the pumpkin pies, which were then quickly pulled off the store shelves.

Our plan is working. Only one more thing left to do.

Late one night, she returned to the same pumpkin patch. This time with her poison powder.

Maglich will make sure they don't grow pumpkins ever again. Maglich is actually doing the people a favor. Now there will be no more sickness from pumpkins. What is that saying about doing a good deed and needing no reward? The only way to stop this sickness is to stop growing pumpkins. Forever. Though a good deed needs no reward, you can thank Maglich.

But while sprinkling the poison, the whispering returned. She decided her boots were still the best way to stop the teasing. And so she stomped. And she stomped.

She stomped until her boots were orange. She stomped until the sun came up. She stomped until the sound of shouting children caught her attention. A small crowd was right outside the patch with their phones out. She had been seen, and worse, photographed.

She rushed home. Packing everything she needed into two suitcases, she drove out of town and vanished.

Several days later, the news ran a story about a missing woman. She was identified as Maggie Lichtenstein and had been caught on security cameras at both the grocery store and the retirement home in connection with a string of poisoned pumpkin pies. The police suspected a connection between this woman and an unidentified cloaked figure caught on film vandalizing a local pumpkin patch. She was described as unstable and dangerous.

Her current whereabouts remain a mystery.

THE CREEPER TRAIN

I t all started with a simple dare. But every single fourth grader (52 in all) had to be in or else *it* wouldn't work. So everyone gathered on the playground after school, each with a home-addressed, stamped envelope. Then, the deck of regular playing cards was shuffled and placed face down on the ground. One by one, each 10-year-old took the top card and slid it—without looking—into an envelope. After all the cards had been drawn and all the envelopes sealed, all the kids walked to the mailbox and dropped them inside.

Today was October 29 and the mail would be picked up the next day, October 30, which meant everyone would receive an envelope on October 31, Halloween. And for 51 of the kids, Halloween Night would be what it's always been: trick-or-treating and costumes. But for the Chosen One, that is, *the one* that finds the Jack of Clubs in the envelope, Halloween Night would be much, much different—possibly even dangerous.

This year Halloween fell on a Saturday, and for Chloe, Saturdays meant guitar; first, taking lessons down the street at the music store, then playing the rest of the day holed up in her bedroom. She walked quickly, guitar case in hand and her long, straight auburn hair blowing wildly in the chilly breeze. Her mailbox stood on a post at the end of the driveway. She looked inside but someone had already brought in the mail.

She went into her room, and after getting her guitar and music situated, Chloe quickly lost herself in the pretty chords and plucked notes. She was startled to hear a knock at her door. Her little sister came in and dropped an envelope on the bed. *The* envelope. The very one she had mailed to herself two days ago. She recognized her handwriting on the outside.

Chloe supposed she might as well open it quickly and get back to playing. After all, this was just a formality and there was nothing to worry about. With 51 other kids also opening their envelopes today, the odds of drawing the Jack of Clubs were low: just one in 52 to be exact.

Chloe tore open the envelope. She saw the red and white decoration typical of the back of playing cards. The wind outside blew some dead leaves against the window. Chloe felt butterflies in her tummy. She took a deep breath and flipped the card over.

The Jack of Clubs stared directly up at her. The little hairs on her neck stiffened straight and chills down her back followed.

This isn't possible. Why me? Chloe wondered as her heart thumped like a drum. Her eyes remained fixated on the Jack. Realization had set in: She was the Chosen One. And tonight, the spookiest night of the entire year, she would have to make good on her word. Oh, how she wanted to call a friend to share the dreadful news but that was against the rules of the dare. Everyone agreed that whoever drew the Jack must keep it secret until Monday when all were back at school.

A tree branch brushing against the window startled Chloe. She put the guitar away and looked outside at the dead leaves blowing in the breeze. Tonight, after sunset, she would go alone to the Creeper Trail to learn if the rumors of it being haunted held any truth.

The Creeper Trail is a "rail-trail," which means it used to be railroad tracks that were removed and replaced with dirt for walkers and bikers. The trail passes through forest and field, crossing bridges and going for miles. Many, many years ago, a train (called The Creeper Train) used to "creep" along the tracks, carrying lumber and ore. The trail was never intended to be walked after dark, but those living near the trail have told of strange sounds late at night.

Out the window, the sun was on its way down. Chloe knew she'd best get going. She put her hair up in a ponytail, grabbed a jacket, and told her parents she was meeting friends to do some trick-or-treating. She had never been dishonest before but tonight she simply *had* to. Secrecy was part of the dare.

Chloe jogged down the street avoiding the shadows and staying in the fading daylight. By the time she arrived at the trail entrance, night had fallen. Alone, she walked the trail hoping her eyes would adjust to the dark, relying on the stars and crescent moon for light.

The woods eventually gave way to an open field. A cow mooed somewhere far away. She crossed a creaky wooden bridge and the trail became woodsy again; the tree branches blocked much of the moonlight.

Chloe decided to turn around and go home. She had walked the trail for long enough to be able to report that the rumors of it being haunted were false. She picked up a rock and placed the envelope with her handwritten address beneath it. It would be her alibi that she had been here and done as promised.

But the instant Chloe took her first step toward home, the wind blew with such ferocity that it kept her from walking. Leaves spun up from the trail and swarmed her head like a hive of angry bees. The ground beneath her began to shake and she couldn't hear her own screams over the wind. Could this be a tornado, roaring louder and getting closer? She curled up on the ground and covered her face.

The next moment, all was quiet and still. Chloe let loose the breath she'd been holding and smelled something burning. She struggled to open her eyes, which stung from the leaves and loose dirt that attacked her moments ago. A dim light came into focus.

She was startled at what looked like a humongous box on the trail. And the box was open on its side and there was a little light inside. Then she saw the wheels. *This is no box. This is a train! But how. . .*

A man with a friendly face and a train engineer's cap poked his head out and extended his hand to Chloe. She grabbed it and he hoisted her up into the boxcar. Inside, she guessed there were 12 to 15 grown-ups and everyone was smiling. Nobody seemed the least bit surprised to see her! The men were standing, leaning against the walls of the train car and the women were seated on hay bales or little wood stools. Everyone seemed to be dressed up for Halloween. The men wore overalls or suspenders and brimmed hats; the women were in long dresses with bonnets.

A couple of them waved to her and Chloe felt instantly comfortable, in this room—or train car—full of strangers.

"So, like, where exactly am I? Are we...?" Chloe asked aloud.

"Why, you're on the Creeper Train, Miss," the man in the engineer's hat said grinning.

"No way! The Creeper Train was shut down forever ago." Chloe felt like Dorothy from the *Wizard of Oz*.

"This train never stopped runnin'. And she never will," the engineer said nodding confidently.

Chloe heard a welcome sound coming from the back of the train car. A bearded man had a guitar and began to play. Another man started to play a banjo. Then, a woman in the corner sat down at a piano and someone else joined in with a fiddle.

The train suddenly jerked forward, knocking Chloe to the ground. And then the singing began.

Creeper Train comin' round,
Pull that throttle to the ground.

Creeper Train rides again,
This fun it won't ever end.

Everyone clapped to the beat. Couples were getting up to dance. One of the men helped Chloe off the floor and spun her around. He let her go in mid-spin, when a woman with a blue bonnet locked elbows with Chloe as the music continued.

This is fun! Chloe couldn't help but laugh as a tall man locked arms with her and led her skipping in a circle. The group repeated the exact same lyrics over and over, but it was catchy. She actually wished her classmates could be here!

Outside, the trees and fields zipped by.

Creeper Train comin' round...

Eventually, Chloe needed a serious break; she was out of breath and her legs felt like spaghetti. But when she tried to stop dancing, one of the smiling men would quickly lock elbows with her and spin her about.

Pull that throttle to the ground...

Even when Chloe tried to sneak away to one of the dark corners of the train, someone grabbed her hand and kept her dancing. She found it odd that everyone had such cold hands. And everyone had terrible breath, like rotting food. Like meat gone bad.

When she was spun to a friendly looking woman wearing a blue bonnet, Chloe was thankful.

"So, when do we get a break?" Chloe shouted over the music. She didn't want to be rude but she did feel a bit of a headache coming on. A glass of water sounded delicious.

The woman smiled at Chloe, a big gaping smile. She didn't have any teeth.

"Never," she replied shaking her head.

This fun it won't ever end....

Chloe wondered if she had, in fact, heard the woman correctly. Did she mean that this same song with the same four lines would keep going? And the dancing too? Surely they would get tired or thirsty.

Creeper Train comin' round, pull that throttle to the ground....

Chloe couldn't handle much more of this; her legs were so tired they could barely stand, let alone dance! But could she jump out of a moving train? That might be the end of her....

Creeper Train rides again....

Every time she tried to scramble away, there was always someone there to make her dance, always with a smile. Ghoulish smiles, she realized. And the train kept moving.

Fighting tears, Chloe shouted as loud as she could, "I can't do this anymore!" Not a single head turned and nobody noticed.

Exhausted, she fell to the ground. This time she swatted away the hands that reached for her and crawled into the shadows of the boxcar. She spotted a guitar case leaning against the corner. Relief. Perhaps they would let her rest her legs if she offered to play.

This fun it won't ever end....

But when she opened the guitar case, it was empty. A man was walking toward her with an outstretched hand. Before he could grab her, Chloe darted over to the guitarist and asked if she could play along. He smiled two rows of dark decaying teeth and handed her the guitar.

He was skeletal-thin; Chloe could see his cheek bones. The moment he let go of the guitar, he stood up and began to sway to the music like a charmed snake. Chloe collapsed onto a bale of hay and quickly set to work learning the three chords of the song. A song she now hated. She'd heard it hundreds of times and it never ended. It never stopped.

I wonder...when do these people eat or drink? They can't really keep going forever. They'll die if they do....

In a millisecond, Chloe understood. She understood who these skinny, smelly, cold people were. She needed to get off this train of death! She looked up from the guitar to see the engineer watching her. He was the only one in the boxcar not smiling. Somehow, *he* knew that *she* now knew.

Chloe strummed the guitar along to the song perfectly and pretended not to notice him. She even smiled at the dancers. One woman smiled back and waved. Chloe noticed the empty gaping sockets in place of her eyes.

Suddenly, the woman frowned and pointed at Chloe, who instantly realized she had played a wrong chord. The train slowed momentarily and then stuttered. One of the dancers tripped over his feet and nearly fell. Chloe had an idea. She purposely played a bad chord. And then another. The dancers looked confused and the other musicians' instruments stopped. The train came to a halt too, just as Chloe hoped it would. The music and the train were in some unexplainable way, related.

Chloe dropped the guitar and made a break for the open boxcar door. Every last ghoulish smile changed to a frown. Cold and bony hands reached for her. When the banjo and fiddle started up again, the train began to move. Chloe had to get out now. The only thing in her way was the engineer standing in front of the open door, arms outstretched like a soccer goalie.

Chloe ran for the door and felt the cold fingers of the engineer wrapping themselves around her wrist. "You're forever a part of this train, Chloe," the engineer said looking into her eyes. "You're one of us now."

Chloe bit down on the skeletal hand of the engineer. Her mouth turned numb but she stayed clamped on his freezing cold hand until he let go. She leaped out of the boxcar and tumbled to the ground. As the train moved down the track, she could see the engineer's face peering out at her. Was he...smiling?

The train soon disappeared and the night became still and quiet again. Chloe got to her feet to run home when she noticed a hat on the ground. It must have fallen off the engineer's head during their tussle.

❦❦

On Monday before school, everyone gathered on the playground to find out who had drawn the Jack and if the dare had been completed. Chloe opened her backpack to reveal the engineer's cap. All eyes widened as Chloe put the cap on her head.

She had expected it to be too big, but it fit perfectly. She had a sudden sense of calm. All the schoolyard noises subsided and she heard one, lone voice. It was the engineer.

Chloe, you're one of us now. Bring your classmates to the train tonight. Remember the music? It is your song now too. This fun it won't ever end....

All 51 classmates waited for Chloe to say something. *Anything.* Chloe smiled and adjusted the cap. "Everyone meet at the train at sunset. You won't believe what I found."

THE VISITOR

I f you ever hear a knock, or a thud, in the middle of the night, it's *never* just nothing. Something or *some being* in the dark made that sound. Well, many years ago, there was a young boy who heard something in the night. First, you need to know a little bit about the place where it all happened. I'll let him tell you himself. Here is Cornelius John Delmby, in his own words. . .

Our family cabin is tucked away very deep in the woods. Nestled atop a small hill protected by dense trees, it sits just above a lake. Our rowboat is tied to the dock, but it doesn't get much use anymore. It's a real pain to put away every year before the lake freezes. Anyway, there are no neighbors for miles.

Finding the cabin is nearly impossible unless you know *exactly* where you are going. When the paved road ends, a gravel road starts and after some miles of twists and turns, the gravel road becomes dirt. Eventually you come upon a small gate with a sign: PRIVATE PROPERTY KEEP OUT. You need a key to open the gate.

As a kid, my favorite time to visit was late October, when trees have pretty colors and nights start getting cold. We usually had the big lake and woods to ourselves during the day and at night we'd sit around and read or play games by the fireplace. There was no television, Internet, or phone service. My parents liked it that way: being invisible to the rest of the world.

It's a small cabin with only a few rooms. My parents had their bedroom at the back of the cabin, and I usually slept in the room off the porch. It was our last night at the cabin that year. I've always been a night owl, so after my parents went to bed, I stayed up to play cards alone in front of the fire. It was stormy out and I heard a soft but repetitive *thud thud thud* coming from outside. A tree branch knocking against the cabin, maybe? The thunder had been terrifyingly loud and the sky had been dropping pails of rain on the cabin for hours.

The thudding noise persisted and grew louder until it sounded like a knock at the door. As I mentioned, we were very much isolated. It was nearly impossible that someone would be outside our cabin at one in the morning in the middle of a thunderstorm.

Was the wind just blowing the old porch door open and closed...open and closed?

But I knew that door had a push-bolt and latch to keep it shut. I needed to find out exactly what was making that noise.

I grabbed a flashlight and slowly opened the main cabin door to peek out onto the dark screened porch. Nothing. So, I went out onto the porch. Lightning flashed. A pair of eyes was looking straight into mine. Thunder cracked.

The visitor was outside on the top step, just on the other side of the screen door. It was an old man, very tall, who wore a dark brimmed hat and long rain coat. When lighting flashed again, I saw his pale face with an expression so tortured, so full of sorrow, that I could feel it.

"Where is she?"

At the sound of the man's haggard voice, I unfroze. The only "she" in this cabin was my mom. I quickly ran to the back of the cabin to wake my parents. My voice wavered nervously while telling them about the spooky old man at the door asking for Mom.

Dad got up. The wood floors of the cabin creaked under his fast and heavy steps. He grabbed the poker by the fireplace as I followed him. Dad flicked on the porch light and stepped through the cabin door. I stayed behind, in the safety of the cabin. Thunder boomed.

"Well, I don't see anything. Looks like you scared away whatever spooky old man you must have been dreaming about," Dad teased me. Another roll of thunder.

"The storm will be over soon. Try to get some sleep," Dad said giving me a gentle pat on the back. I heard him close their bedroom door.

But I knew what I had seen and there was no way I was going to sleep. Not yet anyway. So, I quietly opened the cabin door and peered out into the night. Oh. My. God. The visitor was right there on the steps. My flashlight caught his cool blue eyes staring at me. Did he hide behind a tree when Dad came looking?

"Where is she?" the old man whispered.

"Who is *she*? Who are *you*?"

"She is here. I know she is. Please, tell me where I may find her," his tired voice pleaded.

"I don't know who you are talking about. It's just me and my mom and dad."

The visitor neither moved nor spoke. If this were somehow a dream, I wished it would end.

"Look, I'll give you this flashlight so you can find your way back to the road. It's just over that way." I quickly latched the door after dropping the light on the top step.

Rain tumbled over the brim of the old man's hat. Another flash of lightning. Again I saw his blue eyes: so hollow, so tormented. My spine tingled as he studied me before turning away from the door. I listened as his feet went down the three wood steps and onto the trail. He disappeared in the darkness but even over the rain I heard him humming a song. To this day, I remember it.

Hum hum, hum-da-dee-dum, hum dum hum dum hum-dee-hum-dee-dum

I went back inside and locked the main cabin door. Thanks to the fire it was warm. I remember feeling a bit sad for the strange man. He was probably senile and got lost walking somewhere in the storm.

I crawled into bed and got under about five layers of quilts and wool blankets since mornings were really cold in late October. It wasn't as thundery outside. I wondered about the visitor and why he hid when Dad came out to look for him. What was so special about me?

I was trying to convince myself to sleep when I heard a twig snap right outside the window. Normally, I would have taken no notice but the incident with the visitor had my senses on high alert. So, I lay there in silence, listening. I heard another twig break followed by a rustle of leaves. It was probably just a small animal scurrying for shelter from the rain.

But the dark side of my mind thought it was something more sinister. I wouldn't be able to fall asleep unless I knew for sure. So, I pulled aside a corner of the curtain. There wasn't anything or anyone there. I realized I was holding my breath. I let it all out as I sank back into my fluffy pillow.

Then, there was another rustle of leaves and the snapping of a stick, even closer than before. I yanked aside the curtain. There was the visitor. I went stone cold frozen. I couldn't blink. What did this man want from me?

The visitor put the flashlight I gave him under his chin, which cast terrifying shadows across his pale face, making him look more like...a ghost. I went into complete deer-in-headlights mode. My mouth dropped open but I was too scared to scream.

Then, he slowly cupped a hand behind his ear, and that's when I heard the bells ringing. As they got louder, I caught a melody, a song. It was identical to the old man's humming from earlier.

Hum hum, hum-da-dee-dum, hum dum hum dum hum-dee-hum-dee-dum

The bells continued ringing even as the old man took his hand from his ear and pointed a gnarled finger directly at me. Lightning flashed and a distant rumble of thunder followed. This man wanted something. Specifically from me! I was terrified. Surely his next move was to try to come inside the cabin.

But he didn't. At least not yet. Instead, he shined the flashlight on the ground and set off on the path down the hill toward the lake. Looking out through the bay window, I could follow the old man's flashlight as he moved toward our dock.

Hum hum, hum-da-dee-dum, hum dum hum dum hum-dee-hum-dee-dum

What was the connection between the visitor, this song, and...me? The sound was slowly getting louder. I needed to figure out where the music was coming from and I had to act fast. The visitor might come back to the cabin if he didn't find what he was looking for down by the lake. And, I didn't really want him back at the cabin especially if he was insane.

Hum hum, hum-da-dee-dum, hum dum hum dum hum-dee-hum-dee-dum

The view of the dock was better from the screened porch so I left the safety of the cabin and peered down at the lake. The glow from the flashlight was easy to see in the dark.

The music was even louder out here. I felt the bells pounding inside my head. I shuffled to my right and left to test if the music was louder in a particular direction. While there was no discernable difference in volume, the music seemed to be slowing in speed. Then it stopped altogether.

I was actually relieved until it grumbled to start again. As it did, I felt the smallest vibration on the wood floor. Just a tremble. The music had to be coming from directly beneath me. The crawl space under the porch!

My attention shifted outside. The visitor wasn't on the dock anymore. I could see the little yellow light now zig-zagging along the wooded path. He was on his way back to the cabin.

Without further thought, I grabbed a flashlight, flipped the latches on the porch door, and dashed down the steps into the pouring rain. I crawled through a nasty wet mess of spider webs in the dirty storage space underneath the cabin and followed the sound of the bells. The further I crawled, the louder the bells. I had to be getting closer. I crawled over two life jackets, an oar, and a kayak. Then, I saw it. A glint of silver reflected in the beam of my flashlight. A music box. I crawled over to it. It was partially open and leaning awkwardly against an old tackle box. I reached to snap it shut and the music stopped instantly.

I rushed out of the storage space and found the old man's light now locked on me. He was probably 20 yards away still but moving surprisingly quickly up the path. I took a step toward the cabin door and tripped on a large rock partially buried in the dirt path. I fell to the ground but managed to keep hold of the music box.

The old man was so close I could hear his tortured breathing. Without looking back, I stood up and threw myself up the steps and at the screen door. I screamed as the old man's hand grasped my heel. It felt like an ice pack wrapped around the bottom of my leg. So cold. Unnaturally cold. I kicked my foot free, stumbling up the remaining steps and slamming the porch door closed, locking both latches.

I gasped for breath, my leg stinging with cold and my arm hurting from all of the falling. I sank to the floor cradling my treasure, terrified to move. The old man loomed on the other side of the door. He tugged on the door handle, his eyes, heavy and resigned, never left the music box.

"Open it, please. I want to hear it again," the old man pleaded.

The top was painted with a young couple dancing. There were two names scrawled in the lower right corner. I opened the music box and the bells softly began chiming. I noticed a folded piece of paper sticking out of one of the corners: *Happy Birthday, my love. I found our song! When you hear it, know that I am never far away....*

❦❦

I was always sad to leave the cabin, but this time even more so. I had so much to think about. About halfway home, a song came on the radio that I immediately recognized.

Hey Ho, Nobody Home, Meat Nor Drink Nor Money Have I None

I was about to ask Mom, the family music expert, about it but she beat me to it.

"Did you know this was your great-grandparents' special song? They met when they were just kids on Halloween Night. The song is actually about trick-or-treating. They were married for 60 years. Your great-grandfather actually died on the night you were born," Mom said looking back at me. "You know, you have his eyes."

My mind went back to the visitor. All he really wanted was that music box. I'm glad I gave it to him.

TRICKER? OR
TREATER?

I'm sorry to say that Lumpert Lardy was a very troubled
boy. But he really shouldn't have been. He lived quite com-
fortably in a cozy house by the ocean. His parents worked
hard to send Lumpert to the best schools and the family
always took exotic vacations together in the summer. Why

he didn't turn out to be a nicer boy I simply can't explain. Sometimes, there doesn't have to be a reason, I suppose.

Well, if memory serves me, Lumpert didn't have any friends and he didn't much care for school. Though he was a big kid, he was not strong. He would mostly ignore conversation unless you wanted to discuss candy, for this was his first love. Truly, the boy was obsessed with sweets. On Thanksgiving, he would skip the turkey and stuffing but have thirds of pie and cookies.

So it should come as no surprise that Halloween was Lumpert's favorite day of the year. He loved to trick-or-treat; the goal was always to collect a hoard of candy big enough to last him all year. This Halloween would be no different, though Lumpert was now 14 and a bit old for trick-or-treating. But Lumpert had no plans to stop. And who was going to make him?

So, Lumpert got out of bed at noon, skipping school and making absolutely certain to be fully rested for what he had hoped would be his biggest candy night ever. Needing a costume, he hastily pulled a white sheet off his bed and tore a large hole in the center. He put his head through the hole and let the sheet fall around him. Good enough.

Needing something much larger than those silly plastic pumpkin pails to carry his stash, he fished a large duffel bag from his parent's closet and strapped it on like a backpack. Then, Lumpert dashed out the door in the middle of the afternoon, at least three hours before any other candy collectors.

It didn't bother Lumpert that kids in the passing school buses were giving him nasty looks. He knew they were just jealous that he was getting a head start, and a big one. This meant more candy for Lumpert and less for them.

But not everyone was pleasant when Lumpert came to the door. "Isn't it a bit early?" Or, "Aren't you too old for this?" Or even, "Come back when you care enough to have a real costume," were things Lumpert heard. One woman even tried to slam the door on the boy but was rebuffed when Lumpert pawed his big hand into the candy basket for a fistful of treats.

When the sun started to fall, the streets were busy with trick-or-treaters. One group of little face-painted monsters was heading down the sidewalk toward Lumpert. He refused to let them pass. Like a drill sergeant, he ordered them to empty their pails, one by one, into his huge duffel. Each kid cried when it was his turn. Lumpert just grinned.

By early evening, Lumpert had canvassed most of the neighborhood but still had room in his duffel. He decided to visit the house across the street with no lights on. As you surely know, a dark house means a no-go for trick-or-treating, but Lumpert wasn't going to let anyone off the hook.

There was no answer at the door, but surely they had something sweet? Lumpert took it as a good sign that the door was unlocked. It creaked as he pushed it open.

Inside, all was dark, except for the glow of a lantern showing the way to the kitchen. *How convenient*, Lumpert thought as he strolled forward. Suddenly, from behind him, a deep gravelly voice...

"Trick or treat!"

Startled, Lumpert stopped. Right beside him, dressed in all black, was a man. His face was painted—ghastly white with streaking black tiger stripes. He wore a tall black top hat and his moustache hopped about maniacally as his lips alternated between grinning and frowning.

"I can give you more candy than you've ever dreamed," the man said in a voice so deep it was barely human. Then the man's eyes widened and he began to laugh—the painfully high shriek of an exotic jungle bird.

"I want candy, and I want candy now," Lumpert whined. He didn't like this man, but there was something about him that kept Lumpert enthralled.

The man pressed his nose against Lumpert's and in an unnaturally low voice said, "Then candy you *shall* have."

Lumpert stepped back from the man. "Who are you?"

"Hmmmm. Usually I am The Tricker. But for *you*, I am The Treater." The man moved his eyebrows and moustache up and down as he spoke.

"Just give me my candy and I'll be on my way."

The Tricker produced an orange pail from behind his back. "This is a magic pail. It is...bottomless. Take it and you can have as much candy as you can possibly gather."

Lumpert snatched the pail. The handle was icy cold. Other than that, it was nothing more than the usual orange plastic with jack-o'-lantern face on the front. On the bottom, a sticker read "Made in China." Lumpert saw nothing magical about it.

"I don't want this stupid pail. My duffel is way better!"

The Tricker's eyebrows curled and his lips made a playful grin. Suddenly, Lumpert's bag slipped off his shoulders and dropped to the ground. The duffel unzipped itself and spilled its contents onto the floor. Lumpert dropped to the ground and covered the candy with his body to protect it.

But the candy had other ideas. Every single lollipop, gummy bear, cookie, candy bar, and candy cane playfully danced in the air before disappearing into the "magical" orange pail.

Lumpert looked into the plastic pumpkin and found it to be totally empty. He yelled something inappropriate for this story.

The man with the painted face cackled.

Lumpert was panting, out of breath as if he'd been running. "Where...is *my*...candy?"

The man reached into the pail, far enough that most of his arm disappeared. When he pulled his hand back out, he was holding two suckers and a bag of candy corn. "My dear Mister Lardy, the candy is all here. This is a magical pail. The *only* catch is that no candy can be removed until you're done trick-or-treating and at home. That's how the magic works. Don't worry, even *you* won't fill its depths and the pail will always feel light as a feather. So, run along, Lumpert. Use it to collect as much candy as you possibly can." The Tricker's eyebrows shifted up and down playfully.

"Just how is it you know my name?" Lumpert asked irritably.

"I told you to go, Lumpert. Leave! Or, shall I keep the pail and give it to…"

"No! It's mine! The magic pail is mine now!" Lumpert wiped some drool from his face with the torn sheet he was wearing.

The Tricker's moustache quivered as he grinned. "Now, Lumpert, I expect you'll get hungry again and since you won't have access to the pail's pleasures, here is one treat to keep you going."

Snatching the candy bar, Lumpert studied the wrapper. It had big orange lettering: *Tricker Bar.*

Lumpert rolled his eyes. Walking out of the house, he thought he was *so* above this man's games. *What a fool! Parting with a bottomless magical pail.*

With newfound excitement, Lumpert visited houses at a feverish pace, ringing doorbells and grabbing fistfuls of candy from whomever answered. He hid waiting for younger kids to walk by; then, like a robber snatching an old woman's purse, Lumpert swiped their pails and dumped their candy into his own.

At another house, when nobody answered the door, Lumpert went inside and helped himself to the entire candy basket. The scent of chocolate led him into the kitchen whereby Lumpert stole a full pan of freshly baked brownies.

Just as the Tricker said, the pail never filled and it remained light as a feather.

In a mere hour, Lumpert had successfully banked what was surely a mountain of candy. He had visited every house in the neighborhood. And, just as the Tricker had said, Lumpert got a candy craving. So he devoured the candy bar the Tricker had given him. It was delicious!

Revitalized, Lumpert decided the night was young! He would visit some of the houses across the railroad tracks.

But as he took his first step, the pail became suddenly heavy. *How odd,* he thought. Just a moment ago, the pail was weightless, now he struggled to carry it with both hands. And that wasn't all. Lumpert was hungry again. *Ravenously* hungry. He wished he had another one of those Tricker bars.

Weary from hunger pains and from dragging the now heavy pail, Lumpert plopped himself down on someone's grassy front yard. He tried to flip the pail over and dump some candy, but alas. When he tried to let go of the pail, it was mysteriously stuck to his hands.

Then a familiar voice startled him," Anybody need a ride home?"

It was the Tricker.

"What did you do to me?" Lumpert sounded like he had the flu.

"I just *happened* to be driving by and *happened* to see you laying there. You should be thankful I'm stopping to help you," the Tricker said casually.

He leaned over Lumpert, and as before, pressed his face so close to the boy's that their noses almost touched. The Tricker's icy blue eyes made Lumpert tingle, and his voice was even deeper than before.

"Give. Me. The. Pail," the Tricker growled.

"No," Lumpert whimpered and wrapped his arms around the pail, as if death would result from letting it go.

"I'm only trying to help you, Lumpert. I want to...*unburden* you. Now, give the pail to me."

"Even if I wanted to, which I don't, I can't. It's stuck to my hands," Lumpert replied.

"You don't say?" The Tricker erupted into a raging-hyena laugh. "I can help you, Lumpert, but you must offer it to me for the pail is magical and it believes it belongs to you."

"Okay here, take it then," Lumpert said trying to lift the pail but becoming winded, gasping for air from the effort.

"Thank you, Lumpert." Using a single finger, the Tricker plucked the pail off the ground and tipped his hat to Lumpert as if to say *"What was so hard about that?"* Walking to his car parked on the street, he popped the trunk and placed the pail inside.

"NO!" Lumpert shouted. He struggled to stand but was too exhausted from the ordeal with the pail.

Triumphantly, the Tricker got in the car and lowered his window. "Trick-or-treat, Lumpert Lardy!" he said with another tip of his hat and drove away.

Lumpert buried his face in the grass. He punched the ground with both his fists. Lumpert had collected enough candy to fill his closet. At least a six-month supply. And now it was all gone.

Without that cursed pail stuck to his hands, Lumpert felt his strength return and he was able to walk again. But instead of going home, Lumpert headed straight for the Tricker's house.

The living room was lit by antique lanterns, which created dancing shadows along the walls. In the middle of the room was the largest pile of candy Lumpert had ever seen.

The Tricker was sitting in a chair, elbows on knees and hands locked. "I assume you're here to retrieve your duffel. I left it for you in the kitchen."

"I'm here for my candy," Lumpert said.

A flash of bright lightning in the window behind the Tricker startled Lumpert. It was followed by a clap of thunder. Both unusual for late October.

"Get your duffel and get out of here," the Tricker growled. "I need the rest of the night to sort through this treasure."

"No!" Lumpert screamed, lunging toward the mass of candy piled on the floor.

With magician-like speed, the Tricker swiped the magical pail off the floor and tossed it toward Lumpert lying on the candy pile.

Lumpert saw the pail flying toward him. Fixated, he stared at the inside of the pail but couldn't see the bottom. Just darkness. And the darkness grew as the pail got closer. His body spun in circles and it made Lumpert feel like he was on a very unpleasant carnival ride. He descended into a dark whirlpool. Surrounded by darkness, he fell, and fell, and fell....

Alone again in his living room, the Tricker got to work sorting all of the candy. "Trick-or-treat!"

EPILOGUE

Heard enough, have you? Understandable, the hour is late.

You watch me return the seeds to the orange wall amid hundreds of others just like it. You stand up from the chair and wait for my lantern to illuminate a path to the door. After exiting the Pumpkin Room, you follow me down the long corridor. I bid you on your way as the heavy door to the mansion groans closed behind you.

Soon you are back inside the dark forest and the long walk to whence you came begins. Atop the trees, the stars are shining and your thoughts drift back to the many seeds in the Pumpkin Room. You think a bit about each of the stories you heard. What became of some of those people?

You wonder....You feel, in an unexplainable way, that the stories and characters are part of you now.

You finally get home and crawl into bed. You rest your head on the pillow and something feels, well, unusual. You switch on the lamp. Impossible! How could this be? It's a candy bar. But not just any candy bar, one with big orange lettering: *Tricker Bar.*

ABOUT THE AUTHOR

A lifelong pumpkin fan and ghost enthusiast, Mark Milbrath is thrilled to finally be using his overly active imagination through words and stories. Mark has already had plenty of experience using his imagination through numbers; he's worked for many years as a TV meteorologist and commercial real estate appraiser. He lives with his wife—and potentially knows the exact whereabouts of Maglich—in Northern Virginia. Other than writing, Mark enjoys playing the guitar, tennis, traveling, stargazing, birds, walking in the woods, frequenting pumpkin patches and the occasional late-October haunted activity.

www.facebook.com/Nightforestpress13

Nightforestpress13@gmail.com

CPSIA information can be obtained at www.ICGtesting.com
Printed in the USA
LVOW10s1323171016

509094LV00018B/356/P